EVE'S APPLE

Emma Cooke was born in Portarlington, Co. Laois in 1934. She was educated at Alexandra College, Dublin, and worked in a Dublin office before her marriage. She began writing in the early 1970s and her work has been published both in Ireland and abroad. Her collection of short stories, *Female Forms*, was published in 1981 and her successful first novel, *A Single Sensation*, in 1982.

Emma Cooke has lived in Limerick since 1959.

EVE'S APPLE

Emma Cooke

THE
BLACKSTAFF
PRESS
BELFAST AND DOVER, NEW HAMPSHIRE

First published in 1985
by The Blackstaff Press Limited
3 Galway Park, Dundonald, Belfast BT16 0AN, Northern Ireland
and
51 Washington Street, Dover, New Hampshire 03820 USA
with the assistance of
The Arts Council of Northern Ireland

Printed in Northern Ireland
by The Universities Press Limited

British Library Cataloguing in Publication Data

Cooke, Emma
Eve's apple.
I. Title
823'.914[F]   PR6053.O524/

ISBN 0 85640 350 4 (hardback)
0 85640 344 X (paperback)

For John

I stand outside our house with my latchkey in my hand. Next door, people are leaving a cocktail party.

'Oh go on—you're a devil,' a voice says on the other side of the hedge.

Everyone laughs.

I go into the house. Our oldest child, Anne, is in the sitting-room with Robin. Some time ago she moved out to live with her boyfriend. However, she continues to pay us these visits which are exercises in bewilderment for all of us. Anne's hair is looped up with a twist of blue wool and she looks about sixteen. In fact, she is twenty-two.

The folding doors are open and the baubled Christmas tree winks sharply by the window in the dining-room. It shows up the darkness of the January evening.

It was already dark when I left Billy Black's surgery and other trees winked in houses around the square. I sat for a while outside his place before starting the car. I braced myself with dismissive thoughts, reducing what has happened to a fusion of gametes, and resulting zygotes. Stuff gleaned from biology text-books, which I only vaguely understand.

What I really need is a strong drink. 'Get me a gin and tonic, love,' I say to Robin.

He squints at me. I feel as heavy as the postman's bike.

'Billy Black has confirmed it—I'm pregnant,' I say. I hurl my bag and fur jacket onto an empty chair. Let Anne chew on that as well as Robin. This is grown-up stuff for real. I'm forty-two years old.

Robin stays where he is, standing with his back to the fireplace. He'll catch fire if he doesn't watch out. He starts making those humming noises that show he is upset. A sound as annoying as the buzz of a dying fly.

'Don't do that,' I say, and then feel frightened because I spoke so sharply.

Robin stops with his mouth open, and then he says, 'For Christ's sake—is Billy Black certain?'

I can't wait. I go to the cabinet and get the gin myself. 'Mother's ruin,' I say, lifting my glass.

Anne looks at me as if she is not certain of what I said.

'How did it happen?' Robin asks.

That's great. We've been married for over twenty years and he asks me how it happened. 'Billy Black blames the menopause,' I say.

The three of us brood for a while. Anne slouches back on the sofa, twisting a strand of hair round and round her finger. My own secret opens up like a dark abyss.

I envy Anne, I envy the way she can get up from the sofa, peck us both on our cheeks and say, 'I'll have to leave. Brian and I are having tea in town. We're going to the pictures.' She even puts her arm around my shoulders and gives me a subdued squeeze before tiptoeing out of the room as if leaving a sickness.

I can't help my tears. I sit down on the chair where my fur jacket is, and cry while Robin comes and strokes my back.

'You'll be all right,' Robin keeps saying as I mop my face with his handkerchief.

I must look a mess. Oh, what a kettle of fish, and I wish Robin would stop jiggling his car keys in that irritating way. My Robin is a big softy, so I'm honour bound to make all this as easy for him as possible. Make no mistake about it, I don't want this child to change things between us. Nobody need ever know about Leo— except the priest in the confessional when I go to him with my grievous sins, and there's no rush about that because grievous isn't mortal, it is not in the same class as having an abortion. 'Fuck Religion' the punk junkie had printed on his jacket the last day that I walked down Grafton Street.

I must count my blessings. One—I don't look my age. Robin says he has often noticed that married women don't grow old as quickly as single ones. That's his theory. When I think of his sister, Nancy, I'm inclined to agree. Mind you I'm not sure that this theory applies to men. Nowadays Robin looks much older than I do, almost as old as Nancy. And yet there was a time when there was only one bench between all three of us in the little whitewashed country school—Nancy sitting in the second-class row, and Robin and I with the infants. And even then, I swear, Robin and I were sweethearts, babes in the wood.

Babes. It's so long since I've had a baby. No wonder Billy Black scratched his head. Jenny is fifteen. I haven't had a baby since I was twenty-seven. 'So you and Robin are still going strong,' Billy said, and chuckled. Oh well, that's another thing to thank God for. I definitely thank God that, in spite of Leo, the estrangement between Robin and me has not been complete. We became lovers again in October. But always very carefully, always according to the Billings method and with due consideration to the time of the month. I'm so adept after all these years that I can tell to the very second where the egg is in relation to my Fallopian tubes.

'I'm going upstairs,' I say to Robin. I want to be by myself for a while. 'It's time for the news,' I say, and push the television button for him.

I hardly ever listen to the news. I get too nervous when they show all that shooting and trouble. Our son, Ray, is working in a kibbutz. I don't want to see a close-up of him being lifted onto a stretcher, a piece of cloth being taken to cover his face.

In our bedroom I sit on the edge of the bed. I feel dazed. I feel this unborn child spread inside me like some dreadful hidden bruise, a hurt which I must bear without complaint because I can't face the role of black sheep so late in the day. Oh I'm not going to make a speech about it, but surely a woman who has raised three children deserves to have a quick fling. Even for the good of her health, or to give her a boost by showing her that another man besides her husband finds her desirable. Oh how happy I was. Especially as Leo had been so helpful about the kibbutz—furnishing addresses, making contacts with friends in Israel. Leo said, 'A woman like you shouldn't have to lunch alone,' and he tucked my hand into his raincoat pocket as we ran down the road to the art gallery where the exhibition was being held.

'I don't like them,' I said. In fact I loathed the section showing the war artist's sketches from the trenches. Those skulls. Bits of people sticking up out of the ground. A leg, still wearing its puttee, severed at the knee. 'We'll look at the oils instead,' Leo said immediately. Ever since Ray killed his friend in that silly 'unloaded gun' accident anything that pertains to sudden death upsets me. Especially when the people concerned are eighteen-year-old best friends. 'But you must stop worrying,' Leo said. 'Israel will do him good.'

I hang up my jacket and take off my gold necklace. It's my new necklace, the one that Robin gave me for Christmas. He suggested pearls, but I'm superstitious. Pearls for tears. That bitch Nancy sent me a wallet, probably left over from her summer holiday in Florence, without as much as one lire in it.

I lift the lid of my jewel box and the dancer swivels on her pin. The sentimental waltz tinkles for the umpteenth time. The light over our dressing-table shows up every blotch and line. At least I can smell good. I use the perfume spray, then draw the pink curtains and take off the bedspread. I climb between the sheets for a quick rest. It's cold up here, but blissfully quiet. No one waiting to pounce. No one murmuring, 'I love you just the same.'

If I feel so exhausted now what will I be like by July? But I mustn't think that far ahead, just take it day by day. Billy Black found it all very amusing this afternoon. I suppose I was a bit crazy to think I had started the menopause. 'No such luck,' Billy Black said, grinning hard at my comical dismay. The whole business seems so unimportant as I lie here on my side of the double bed. All I have to do to ensure the success of the undertaking is to keep my mouth shut. This is my baby, and no one else's. I close my eyes and try to concentrate on blackness to help myself relax. All the colours in the spectrum whirl beneath my eyelids. Well, I never actually believed that the menopause was making my breasts grow tender, or causing my early-morning queasiness. 'Anyway, it's wonderful to be alive,' that is what my father always said when things were not going well. Of course, he isn't alive anymore. Even so, I remember the words and they help.

Wonderful. Wonderful. Wonderful to wake up and find I have

been having a bad dream, that I just imagined last Friday in Dublin, with the wind and rain blowing in my face as I headed down the street towards Leo's office. I don't even know why I travelled up, or what I had expected Leo to do. (I had already written him several letters but had not sent them.) It was a biting cold day, with people bundled up like unsavoury parcels, in sodden coats and dripping hats. And a woman nearly poked my eye out with the spoke of a broken umbrella. 'I can wait,' I said to the secretary in Leo's office, and sat oozing on a chair while the girl tapped her ghoulish plum fingernails on the typewriter keys. I stared her down, refusing to be sneered at. Later, I called Leo's office from the railway station, but he was still unavailable. Perhaps I wished to leave a message? No. It was a day I preferred to leave unrecorded. On the train I realised that I had left behind me a damp bag containing a Bewley's cherry log. The thought of its discovery by that spiky painted secretary rankled like a public shaming.

Today the weather is also horrible. Even with the curtains drawn I can hear the trees on the road swishing their branches. Bloody January. Bloody aftermath. I hear someone banging about on the landing. Judging by the racket—the rowdy transistor and the slammed door—it's Jenny.

And now Robin is here in the room. I keep my eyes shut when he switches on the bedside lamp. I don't want to watch him changing his trousers. I know every sinew and knob of his body. Not that he's skinny. In fact he's developing quite a paunch. And he doesn't need to get his hair cut very often—it's sparse enough as it is. 'I wouldn't want to cause any trouble between you and Robin,' Leo said, 'because I think very highly of him.'

'Alright, pet?' Robin whispers.

'Just tired,' I drawl as Robin tucks the edge of the sheet under my chin. Cuckold. The dirty words for men are as bad as the ones for women—cunt, bitch, whore, tramp *versus* bollocks, bugger. Oh, the prehensile toes of Leo's baby are hooked onto my soul. I know that it's Leo's baby. Let's skip the preliminaries and say it has to be, because with Leo I never bothered about charts, temperatures or examination of vaginal mucus.

No rest for the wicked. It was hardly worthwhile taking off my dress, I tug it on again and go downstairs.

In the kitchen I try to think of something original I can conjure up for three people from five eggs, a carton of cottage cheese and a packet of orange juice. I tell myself that food is just food and that most of the world thinks itself lucky to get a bowl of rice per day. I put four of the eggs on to boil, two for Robin, and set the table with a family hodge-podge of different-coloured crockery.

My dress is already too tight at the waistline. And I suppose it will be the same with the rest of my wardrobe—my good suit, my lace cocktail dress, the velvet outfit I foolishly bought in a sale—every rag I possess gone west in the cause of idiocy. Oh, I shouldn't have let Robin suspect anything. I should have taken off to London on some pretext. Invented a prodigal brother or a rich auntie. Except that Robin knows everyone that I know—including Leo. Once I told Robin about my symptoms I was sunk—he would never agree to an abortion. I could talk about zygotes, the embryo, the organism, a woman's rights, until I am blue in the face. If I wanted to get rid of the baby I should have thrown myself under the train last Friday instead of climbing onto it—minus my cherry log.

'If you can't be good be careful,' that's what Bel used to say to my father whenever he was going off on one of his rare sprees. Of course men can get away with anything. Creeping off to their conferences, and fishing trips, getting up to all kinds of tricks and no repercussions. Not that it means I have any excuse for my lack of clear-headedness, my abandoning of years of scepticism. I have always accepted the rules inflicted by my state in life, otherwise so much of it would seem superfluous—like the meringue on a lemon meringue pie. It has all been much more than empty activity. I believed from the beginning in the rightness of marriage, the rightness of my marriage—and of Paul and Geraldine's too. 'Sometimes I know all this is turning me into a moron,' Geraldine said once. We were sitting in her pale green and primrosey kitchen, sipping chilled white wine. I miss Geraldine a great deal. She had so much energy. Leo would have admired her.

According to Leo, he had never slept with a woman before he married Hester. He believes in marriage as much as any of us. This, the fact of his marriage plus his decision not to rock boats, has given him *carte blanche* ever since, turned infidelity into the great excitement of his life. I could find no answer to his arguments. And look what happened.

The only solution is to attend to the next job—and the next. Switch off the ring under the egg saucepan, plug in the kettle. Jenny wants a frozen pizza instead of an egg, but she can't have a frozen pizza.

'Well I don't want a boiled egg,' she says, taking two slices of bread from the wicker basket and jamming them into the toaster.

She is a flurry of cheesecloth and wild hair. She smells of sandalwood and something else.

'You've been smoking,' I accuse.

'No I haven't. Cross my heart!'

'Listen duckie . . .' I try.

But she squirms away from my outstretched hand, picks up the milk jug and drinks from its rim. She's lucky that her father saves her skin by coming into the kitchen. I'm ready to let fly.

Although nowadays one has to be careful, remember that young people are at risk, practice understanding. Take drugs—take that snippet in the paper I read on the train. An eleven-year-old schoolgirl gave birth to a boy, here in dear old Ireland. Her identity was safeguarded by welfare workers. Well, who'd want to know? And if Jenny isn't smoking, who is? A specimen with spiky hair and one earring? One of the Russian airmen who lodge up the road and are easily recognisable with their oily leather jackets? *Lolita*— that was a Russian imagination. Or some wily soft-soaper with no language barrier, only Jenny's bluejeans to conquer. A smoothie like Leo. A bugger—using the word in a general rather than a particular way.

Forget it. Fill teapot. Everyone sit down. Must get hair set tomorrow. There's a fruitcake in the tin. Yes, I'm exhausted.

Look at these maternity clothes. They're all so hopelessly out-of-date they'd make you scream. Not even tinkers would touch them.

It must be years since I've opened this drawer. I hardly ever come into Ray's room. It's too empty, too uninhabited. And I broke a fingernail tugging the heavy drawer of the old chest.

Don, who was Ray's best friend, is dead. Even when all the formalities were over and it was quite clear that it had just been an unfortunate accident—nothing to incriminate Ray . . . the gun shouldn't have been there . . . no one knew it was loaded . . . it hadn't been used for years . . . it was a miracle it hadn't gone off before this . . . a faulty catch . . . rust—it didn't alter the fact that Don was dead. 'You didn't kill him,' I must have said it a thousand times and all I got was, 'It was only meant to be a joke, Mum.' That's the way it is when you've had a terrible shock. You keep saying the same thing over and over, but every time it sounds different. 'It was only meant to be a joke, Mum.' A joke? Don was Paul and Geraldine's only child.

'It was only meant to be a joke, Robin.' And, after all, my joke will end in gain rather than loss.

This floppy lavender smock doesn't look half-bad, even if it does stink of mothballs.

'What's wrong?' I asked when I came home and Ray met me on the doorstep. It never even dawned on me that the police car on the road had anything to do with us. When he told me about Don I was so shattered that I expected I'd faint. But I didn't. Instead I punched him. He felt as cold and strange as one of those ancient standing stones.

Ray's altar-boy outfit is packed away under my maternity things.

I can still see him and Don up on the altar with Monsignor. A pair of quaint boy-penguins, paddling about in their black slippers. Myself sitting in a front pew and agonising because I know by the sniffles that Ray has forgotten his hankie again. 'My brothers and sisters, we are gathered together . . .' My husband, my daughters, my son, my friends.

I had no brothers and sisters. That is, I was an only child. An only, motherless child to make it worse.

All I had of my mother was the knowledge that she had been given the biggest funeral the town had ever seen. Partly because her family owned half the place, but more particularly because she had been an actress of sorts before she came back from the city and married my father. Two well-known stage personalities stepped off the Dublin bus to follow her coffin. One of them—a man in a cape—was definitely wearing lipstick; the other one—also a man—recited a poem beside the open grave.

I got all that information from Bel Hanratty. Bel was my father's friend and companion. I can remember as far back as the day she moved into our house. I was still very young—not even started school. The day before there had been a huge woman with bandaged legs and little starry flowers on her apron, fighting and banging as usual with the black smoky range in the kitchen. Now I was standing beside a huge boxy suitcase in our hall—thinking that I'd fit inside it—and a dull red swirly coat that smelt of Bel Hanratty was hanging on a hook in the hall beside my father's rubber mackintosh.

I didn't mind at the time. Bel was jolly and quick. And her shortsleeved dresses were bright as flowerbeds, and she let me play with her scarlet lipsticks, and try on her turbans, and put my little feet into her wedge-heeled sandals, and clapped her hands when I went staggering around the sitting-room.

She was usually in good humour. Except on the days that she got the letters with the English stamp. She always used her breakfast knife to open those letters. It was my job, when I was small, first to clean the blade of the knife with a scrap of paper. On wet days the letter was a soggy lump in my hand when I got it from the postman, and I was always afraid that it would dissolve the way snowballs did before I got down to the breakfast-room. It was the only piece of interesting mail that ever came to our house. It made the curlers rattle in Bel's hair. 'That . . . that . . . that . . .' she'd say, crumpling up the pages in her hand. 'Now Bel, watch out,' my father would say, pulling me between his thighs and locking his fingers in front of me like a gate. 'That . . . that . . . that so-and-so,' Bel would say. Afterwards she'd spend most of the day resting and I'd have my father all to myself.

Eventually her husband, who had gone over to live in Camden, died. But I suppose by that time she and my father didn't think it worth their while to get married.

The King family lived down the hill from our house. Robin and Nancy and their parents. Their house was just as big and gloomy as our own, with almost as many unused rooms.

One day I was playing beggar-my-neighbour with Robin at the table by the parlour window in the Kings' house when I heard Mrs King say, *sotto voce*, to a visitor, 'Look at the way she parades herself.' I looked out onto the street and all I could see was Bel, on the opposite footpath, walking past the Christian Brothers' school. She was wearing her new toque with the diamanté clip instead of her usual turban. I guessed that Mrs King didn't like Bel any more than Bel liked her.

'That old cat,' Bel called Robin's mother. It wasn't a bad description of Mrs King, who spent most of her time wrapped in moulting woolly shawls, sitting on her parlour sofa, eating bits and pieces off trays and studying the racing pages for her daily flutter.

But there was nothing feline or fluttery about Mr King. He was all polish and sharp edges. When he marched into the room that day everyone straightened up. Robin and I suddenly settled the playing cards into one neat pack. Mrs King gave her shawls a sharp tug, pulled up from her cushions for a moment and offered her cheek to be kissed. The visitor said that she hadn't realised it was so late, and got up to go. That's what came of dressing yourself in a neat pinstripe suit, as Mr King did every morning, and going out to manage the best shoe department in Ireland. (The shoe department was only part of Hurley's drapery store, but there was no use in looking for shoes anywhere else.)

'Good morning, Mr Stone, and I see you have your little girl with you today.' To which my father replied, 'I know you're the man to advise me, Mr King.' I shifted from one foot to the other, feeling a fool. 'Hem, hem. Now, let me see.' There was not a flicker of a smile on Mr King's face, no recognition that I had been playing cards with his son the day before when he came home from work, and would probably be there again later. 'And what does the young lady have in mind?' Mr King asked. I had seen a beautiful pair of blue and cream wedge-heeled sandals, my heart's desire, in the small shop on the square. The shop that Bel went to. 'Oh, something good for school, I suppose,' my father said. 'Ah, yes.' Mr King already had one of the girls from the ladies' counter climbing a ladder and taking down boxes. Big white boxes, thick brown shoes. 'No. I can't really recommend the fringed tongues,' Mr King said. 'Dr Phillips's wife likes this plain leather brogue for her girls,' *et cetera, et cetera.*

It was a crashing blow for Mr King when Hurley's went out of business. However, that wasn't until years and years later. Robin and I were well married by then. Anne and Ray were very young, Jenny was a baby and my father and Mrs King were dead.

When I eventually had the job of telephoning Nancy to tell her that her father was now also in heaven, I felt it was easy for her to crumple, sobbing on the floor of her apartment. She hadn't been through what I'd been through. Ten months of her father down at the breakfast table before any of us. In the same old pinstripe suit. A brief respite when he walked down the road to the local church for ten o'clock mass. But the rest of the day, conscious of him sitting tight in the corner, sombrely watching me while I tried to keep myself from climbing the walls.

And here's the silver teapot to prove it.

I said, 'You shouldn't have done that, Mr King. We don't want anything.' 'It's a very good teapot,' he insisted petulantly. The teapot was given to Mr King by the Hurleys after he had worked in their shop for forty years. It had an inscription on the side. 'I was never sick a single day in my life,' Mr King said. 'Well, I can always use it for picnics,' I said, giving the teapot a little flourish to

emphasise my joke, and unfortunately banging the spout against
the sideboard.

'But that's fantastic,' I wept, when Robin insisted that his father
had good cause to believe I'd done it on purpose. 'The day my
father started work he was fourteen years old. On the morning of
his first day there the town band walked in front of him, playing
music, the whole way from his own house to Hurley's. What do
you mean the teapot is only dinged?' he shouted. 'Your mother
never even had that teapot polished,' I yelled. All my life I'd been
hearing Mr King tell the story about the band and its music.

Things were not so good but we got over it. It wasn't that I
disliked Mr King, but having him living with us made life too
complex, too convoluted.

Ten months can be a very long time. So can nine months.

'I can only stay a second,' I said to Leo.

I don't know what I'm going to do.

'He saw his little girl happily married to a nice Catholic boy of
good background before he died, thanks be to God,' Fr Bussey said
about my own father.

My father died suddenly while Robin and I were on our
honeymoon. A waiter came and hammered at the bedroom door
in the middle of the night, shouting the news. It woke up everyone
else in the *pensione* too, and there was great excitement.

When I managed to get home I found Bel Hanratty in our house
all by herself. My father's coffin had been taken to the church. All
the funeral arrangements had been made. After a while Nancy King
arrived with a message from her mother, saying that I must come
down and stay with them, that I'd be able to sleep in Robin's bed.
I was glad I wouldn't have to stay with Bel. She was full to the brim
with tears that didn't fall and I was terrified of saying something
that would make them spill over.

I went down to the Kings' and soon afterwards Fr Bussey called.
Mrs King actually struggled off the sofa and hobbled out of the room,
leaving us on our own. 'And soon you'll be bringing forth children
yourself,' Fr Bussey said, giving me a sideways look, after we'd
passed some more remarks about my father. 'Robin won't be home
until next week,' I blurted out. I was almost as upset about Robin,

left behind in Rome, as I was about my father. And he was broke because we'd used up almost all our money to pay for my airline ticket. The whole thing seemed like a sell-out. And I wouldn't be able to wear my lovely 'going away' red pill-box again for ages. The Hurleys had sent up a selection of neat black outfits with sensible hats to match.

I felt stranded. Like the person that no one can place in the old family photograph. Although I suppose that was Bel's role. But she didn't even come to the church for the requiem mass, or show up in the cemetery. Not a sign of her anywhere.

I called back up to the house to see her on the day that Robin arrived to collect me. We were heading straight for Limerick, where the insurance company had given him a house to go with the job. 'Do you want to come in, Angel, and have a look around?' Bel asked. I shook my head. I'd come back in a few weeks time when she was gone. 'Keep your chin up kiddo,' she said, and gave a laugh that sounded like a spoon being rattled in a tin can.

Meanwhile, where was Leo? I know as much about a Jewish boyhood as I do about the war in Vietnam, or the war in the Middle East for that matter. All I care about is that no one drops a bomb on my son, Ray.

'Ray has gone to Israel,' I said to Bel the last time I visited. I'd never told her about the accident with the gun. Bel, kept warm by the nurses, looked comfy enough. A hot-water bottle on her lap under the rug, a woolly hat and the white socks I brought her last year. 'Israel! Where's Israel?' Bel asked. 'Out foreign,' I said. (I always have to look at an atlas to get it right.) The red wig Bel wears nowadays stuck out in loops from under her woolly hat.

I've heard that wigs play a big part in Jewish women's lives.

I once saw a waxen-faced woman trying to set fire to a red wig in the cloakroom of a Limerick hotel. I was afraid to stare at her directly so I watched her in the mirror. She was ready to commit murder. She'd been one of hundreds who'd travelled miles in answer to a hoax advertisement in the local paper. It said that a number of red-haired women were required to take part in a film about Ireland. Word had spread and people were coming from all directions to look and laugh at all the red-haired April fools. Robin and I were just there by accident.

Bel's loopy wig made her look like somebody's old golden cocker. She even said things like, 'Why don't they take me out and shoot me?'

You can belong to any race or nationality in the world and also be a Jew. Karl Marx was a Jew and so was Sigmund Freud. The showbiz man, Sammy Davis Junior, is as black as the hob and Jewish. The President of Israel is an Irishman. And Robert Briscoe, Lord Mayor of Dublin, was Jewish.

We didn't talk about Limerick to Bel.

There haven't been many Jews in Limerick since the early part of this century when a Redemptorist priest started a pogrom. He blamed some Jews who lived in the city for the misfortunes of the poor. Leo hated Limerick, but I like it here. 'I'd rather go to my favourite uncle's funeral than go to Limerick,' Leo said. Leopold Bloom, most famous character in modern fiction, was a Jew. I spent every morning of one wet August lying in a lumpy bed in Kilkee reading *Ulysses*. The month was up before I got to the famous Molly Bloom bit and the book had to go back to the library. 'I'm not a Limerick person, so don't take it out on me, Leo,' I pleaded. 'You live there, you educated your children there,' he accused.

He saw problems where none existed, displayed an anger which I found contrived. I see now it was just another ruse to keep me in my place. All that pogrom stuff is ancient history. And now, if he only knew, it's his baby that is due to be born in July, his baby who is going to be taken down to Monsignor and turned into a Christian. Ha! Ha! That's how important a father with a strong sense of history is.

And this is what happens to a woman who goes on a spree. She comes home, prepared to cover her tracks. Next thing she knows, here's the whole mysterious business landed on top of her, waiting for her to solve it. And all I can do is potter around. Try to relax for heaven's sake. Tell myself that maybe it is going to work out. Ask Betty, the next time she comes, if she can give me a few more cleaning days per week to help me restore order after chaos, keep the cobwebs at bay.

Almost as soon as we arrived in Limerick, Robin was earning enough money with the insurance company for us to have a woman in the house. I'd never have managed otherwise when the children were small. I'd have blown my brains out. On birthdays I was free to see that everything went smoothly for Ray and his little pals, especially Don. 'Teddy Bears' Picnic' on the record player, and bingo in the kitchen. Gallons of lemonade. Potato crisps, sausages and buns.

They were small happy notes in the smooth existence in which I pattered around with mittened innocence while out there somewhere women of a different breed were clenching their fists and burning their bras. I was not interested in their preachings. Bel was all I ever needed to know of the unorthodox. I did not want to become like Bel. She is definitely not my type.

Over the years I blocked my ears and concentrated on getting the house right. Eventually it was perfect. Here's the dining-room, with its magnificent suite as evidence. To tell the truth, the room is too small and dinner parties are acrobatic feats. But that old silver teapot with the twisted spout is a family heirloom. And look at the claw legs on everything. They take almost an hour to polish, and several tons of elbow grease.

'I don't believe in messing around,' I said to Leo when he first asked me if he could meet me on my own. I had been attending a conference with Robin. It was shortly after everything happened and Geraldine and Paul were moving house. Of course I was pleased, standing there in the acres of plush and gilt. It meant I was looking good, not white-haired and frumpish like some of the women. Leo's wife was not with him. 'This isn't Hester's style,' he said. OK, I was a fool to feel grateful. I'm sorry now that I listened to the compliments he plopped out like sweets from a vending machine. They're not much use to me here, back in the family circus.

If he'd even drop me a line, send me a thinking-of-you card, or even a 'furry-friends' telegram all dressed up in a fuzzy costume.

When I was a schoolgirl I had an English pen-pal whose hobby was the theatre, especially the Old Vic. I wrote that my hobby was embroidering handkerchiefs. I bought a plain white one, lady's size, in Hurley's, made a cross-stitch border all around the edge, and sent it to her one Christmas. She sent me some old theatre programmes, which Bel threw on the fire.

Oh, in the weeks ahead I am going to continue to keep my ears blocked, my mittens on. There will be gossip enough as it is without making it a gloves-off situation. 'Poor Angel.' 'I think it's atrocious.' 'You'd think they would use something.' 'I wonder was it her idea or the husband's?' 'After all the trouble she has had—that accident, the boy.' 'And of course that other business—her own best friend.' 'Personally, I always thought Geraldine was a bit of a nymphomaniac.' And it all ending up as usual in high-pitched cackling.

Edna will be secretly delighted. She takes the pill—she doesn't trust the Billings method. 'And I'm going to keep right on taking it until I'm at least sixty—unless Tony dies.' That's Edna. She is the nearest thing I have to a friend since Geraldine left.

Supposing Robin was dead? But he's not, I fluster. And he isn't laid up or recovering from a major heart attack like May Murphy's husband, tottering along the road with the aid of a stick. Robin looks perfectly capable of impregnating me. He is perfectly capable.

Thank God I'm not a widow! What a lamentable state of affairs that would be. Oh, I can see all the faces perking up over the china cups. Another little domestic mystery solved. 'So that's what took her to Dublin so often last autumn. I always wondered about that "friend". I couldn't understand why she had to stay overnight when there is a late train.'

Noelle I called my imaginary Dublin friend. I used to talk a lot to Edna about Noelle, this make-believe creature with whom I claimed to have shared my schooldays. I invented a series of rather comical disasters and mishaps for her, and talked about them so convincingly that Edna asked lugubriously after I had made one of my trips, 'And how is our friend in Dublin?' I even made up stories about this Noelle for my own amusement while I travelled down on the morning train. Noelle. What made me call her that? Why not something smarter—Clara, Moira.

Noelle and Leo, it is as if both of them are figments of my imagination now.

Going into his bedroom was an extraordinary experience. The air was full of delicious undercurrents. I expected everyone belonging to me to come crawling out from under the bed, or to burst out of the *en suite* bathroom singing as if it was a surprise party. Oh, it was so much more exciting than talking about who met who last week in Kilkee, or cooing over photographs of May's baby granddaughter. Granny May. Granny flats. Oh Jesus—I'll be next! After so many years I can't even remember what it was like. I had my children when I was far too young. Jenny is fifteen. 'My baby,' Leo took me in his arms, 'that sultry look of yours does things to me.' If he could see me now!

Here I am, growing older by the minute as I try to figure out how I got myself into this jungle. Fact—the zygote contains the genetic code required for development. Source—Anne's biology books, or the correspondence columns of the *Irish Times*, I can't remember which. It makes no difference. I can't understand such technicalities. Although I'm sure it has to do with whatever sparked so briefly between Leo and me. And now I am its slave.

Up and down in the train. Up and down. Heuston—Colbert—Heuston—Colbert—Heuston. I ignored the undercurrents when I came home after my second visit in a week. I got up at the crack of dawn so that I could have my hair set before catching the train in Limerick. Then in Dublin I bought a present for May's baby granddaughter in a Henry Street shop. And, when I got home, I brought it round to the young mother who sat sighing over her woolly bundle in May's spotless kitchen. 'Did you ever see such a baby?' May asked.

Wait until they see this one.

Unfortunately, the toy I bought was all sharp edges and probably toxic as well. 'Made in Hong Kong, I'm afraid, Angel,' May said, putting on her tired voice as she stored the bauble in an out-of-the-way cupboard. It would have been more honest to put it in the dustbin directly. 'It must be lovely to get up to Dublin on your own, Mrs King,' the daughter, Francesca, said. I knew what she meant. Kids. Kids plus husband, and not a minute to yourself for years and years. And then, suddenly, one day—zoom. 'Oh life is one long cocktail party for Angel,' May said. She didn't mention Anne.

If Francesca had tried living in sin May would have died of mortification—and rage.

I hate them nowadays—cocktail parties, I mean. Even so, I go along, and to other functions—*smörgåsbord*, fashion shows, charity auctions, flower-arranging demonstrations, race meetings, antique fairs. I'm not boasting when I say that Robin and I are very popular and get asked to everything. Of course, now and again, in spite of overcrowding and the stifling heat, everything turns out to be good fun. It goes OK, and I feel pleased with myself.

Then it is almost like the old days—like that night at the medieval banquet with Paul and Geraldine. There was a special kind of unity between the four of us, and it was one of the best nights that the castle had had for a long time. The hostesses were huge gorgeous butterflies, and everyone was having a good time. Some Frenchmen sat opposite us, and Geraldine and I giggled at each other's French while Robin and Paul tried sign language. When I saw Robin reach over and stroke Geraldine's shoulder I swallowed the demon frog in my throat, resisted the urge to howl like the banshee. It wasn't worth it.

Oh I wish Geraldine was here to rescue me, to have a good laugh. I shared everything with Geraldine—even Robin. I never held anything back. Since she left town my socialising has become haphazard, nomadic.

At the time of the rumpus I didn't react like Paul. He behaved like a pig. When he had said and done everything he could think of, he systematically smashed the geranium pots on the front steps and in the porch, while Geraldine yelled, 'You must be out of your Chinese mind.' She said I was great to be so forgiving. I didn't find it difficult. I understood that what had happened had been a transient thing. Robin was mine. And I didn't want to lose my best friend. Then there was the horrible accident, and her only son was dead.

Soon after that Paul asked his firm to give him a transfer. He was moved to Killarney almost immediately. Geraldine wrote to say that the view from their house was glorious, and that the patio would be terrific for sunbathing. We had always sunbathed in each other's gardens. I took a deeper tan than she did. It was almost a relief when they left, there was so much we didn't want to think about. It was nobody's fault. Everyone was most emphatic on that point. 'You've just got to accept it, Angel—please!' Geraldine begged. 'It was just—just fate.' But that didn't solve the problem. She and I had been such friends, even knew each other's birthdays and sent funny cards. 'We're the perfect age—between baby fat and middle-aged spread.' 'At our age it's easy to avoid temptation, but it's just as easy to go and look for it.' 'So you're twenty-nine again!'

Forty-three next birthday—that's no joke. That's not so marvellous. That's what comes of getting married at nineteen and having Anne right away. A baby when I'm twenty and another when I'm forty-two. It's enough to make a woman depressed about sex and wish she was frigid. Especially when she has never played around in her life before. Except for a kiss or so at a dance, perhaps, as compensation for the deadly grinding marathon of speeches about the building industry, or the insurance industry, or government policy—nothing more. Only because I was wearing the white dress with the beaded bodice—which I bought in that marvellous new boutique where everything costs a fortune—and felt it deserved a tribute. Also, my head was swimming from the wine. No one cared. Even Edna—whose husband was the one who kissed me—laughed.

Soon I won't have a stitch that fits. Just cupboards full of unwearable clothes going out of fashion while I paddle around in loose garments, getting swollen feet and piles. Isn't that terrific. When I'm pregnant I grow huge. After six months I have to look in a mirror if I want to see my toenails.

All I need now to complete the pleasant prospect is a visit from my sister-in-law, Nancy. Nancy sitting on the sofa, clicking her teeth, her neat briefcase of conference papers resting neatly beside her. That's how a woman becomes important nowadays—she attends seminars and conferences *ad infinitum*. Or so it would seem from listening to Nancy. And I sit, all simpering smiles, hoping that the glaze doesn't evaporate from my eyeballs, hoping I won't open my mouth too wide and call her a withered-up bitch.

Even her clothes are all wrong. The last time I saw her she had ruined that expensive grey dress by pinning a huge pink rose where modesty vests used to go.

Not that she cared. All Nancy cares about are her conferences, and her seminars, and her game of golf. Lady Captain Nancy King. And keeping herself decent, hiding her boobs with silly satin flowers. You don't have to be a fortune-teller, or even very bright, to foretell Nancy King's future. More golf, more seminars, more women's committees. No men. There haven't been any men for years. The last one I can remember was a hairy old ballad singer who, it turned out, had a wife and a clatter of kids. I burst out laughing when I heard that titbit. It took my mind off the bad news—strikes, more awful demonstrations, more trouble in the North.

If I can continue to tick over like this, thinking of my friends, my sister-in-law, and so on, I'll survive. I'll bear the brunt all on my own. I'll get through the present crisis without making headlines. 'Limerick mother's "love-life" sets off major row in business circles'. Leo's company is one of Robin's biggest clients— unfortunately. And as well as having business links, politically they're both in the same camp. They're in agreement on who should run the country. They both definitely want a clause put into the Constitution so that no woman can have an abortion in Ireland under any circumstances. And here I am—Robin's wife having Leo's baby. Never mind, I heard that Leo spoke well at the last Rotary Club luncheon on the need to guarantee the right to life of the unborn. They are not the words of a jealous lover. That's not perverse sentiment thrown out by an unscrupulous man.

All my maternity dresses look so antiquated. How about this old, old one with the frill? Hideous. I wouldn't wear it to a dog fight.

When Robin kisses me I feel as chilly as the Snow Queen, but I'll nurse that secret splinter of ice in my own heart. I'll pass off my disgruntlement as pregnancy blues.

I'll keep my mind occupied elsewhere with television serials and library books full of cultured well-to-do women over forty, husbands and their mistresses, simpletons of twenty-five with god-like bodies. All that sensuous, dramatic and wryly humorous stuff.

All those messages from another planet about aggression, tenderness, lust, passivity, ambivalence, hostility—the lot. I might even take up bridge playing again in spite of the fact that I'm eleven weeks pregnant. In America, a baby born prematurely at eleven weeks (alternatively, a fertilised zygote born prematurely at eleven weeks) survived, and is now a normal healthy child. I might as well do something besides sit around and chat. Play bridge, keep my nose buried in those confusing novels, go to mass every morning, go to the station and watch the train pulling out for Dublin, hoping and praying that my brain doesn't split.

When I was a child there was a man living in the town who had two wives. One of them was an ex-wife but claimed equal right to the title and benefits. When the man died both wives attended his funeral and stared into each other's faces across the grave. Rival wakes had been held—one in the town's chief hotel, the other one in the man's house. Many people went to watch and listen at both, but nobody could discover the exact state of the man's affairs. Not even the parish priest.

In time everything sorts itself out. This time next week . . . next month . . . next year. One hundred years from now we'll all be dead. Christening, First Communion, Confirmation, Marriage, Last Rites. Even the unborn child will have gone through all the actions, this egg that incubates as I turn my face to the wall.

Up and down to Dublin—up and down. If I telephoned Leo and explained everything, would he arrange a state reception for me? A big 'do' in Dublin Castle, with a government minister or major diplomat to take me by the arm and introduce me to the principal guests. Or how about the Papal Nuncio. 'My Lord, I would like you to meet Angel King, a lady who will not take the abortion trail.' 'Mr Editor, this is the woman who refused, in spite of conditions that many of us would consider impossible and the National Union of Journalists, to consign her unborn child to the refuse sack.' 'We are gathered here to pay tribute to Mrs Ireland 1983—Angel King—the person who most clearly reflects the genuine and individual desires of the people.' He would in his hat. Or perhaps if I wrote him a note suggesting that we should meet and get the situation straightened out. No, no use. Because there is no situation—and nothing to do but breeze along.

I leaf through the papers and what do I find? 'She agreed for £6,000 to bear the child for a New York businessman whose wife was infertile.'

And anyway, Leo would probably refuse to believe me.

And £6,000 wouldn't get me very far. I haven't any money of my own. My father had nothing put away for a rainy day, or for his only child. He'd just been scraping along. After he died we sold up the house, I gave Bel a few scraps of furniture, debts were paid, and that was that.

Oh, Edna is right. A woman should stay on the pill until she's sixty. They're only throwing sand in your eyes when they tell you it's dangerous. Everything is dangerous—even going to bed is dangerous. A woman could wake up and find a rapist on top of her. Even in that case there could be no justification for an abortion. You just can't sweep the unborn under the carpet and hope they won't squeal.

It was Billy Black who suggested the Billings method when I told him that I'd been bleeding every day for weeks. Jenny was a year old and I had been trying the pill. 'Of course Robin will have to put on the brakes until you're able to work it out properly for yourself. After that there's nothing to worry about.' That's what Billy Black said. He has never met Leo.

Just before Christmas I tried the hot bath plus the bottle of gin trick. Afterwards I felt remorseful. It seemed as bad as an attempted assassination. I wondered if it was a sin I should tell in confession. But the words were too complicated and the baby is still alive.

It can sleep in my cradle. The cradle is one of my few meagre heirlooms. A simple wooden affair on rockers, that was made by a carpenter friend of my father's. It has stood on our rather small and cramped landing ever since Jenny grew out of it. You can usually find yesterday's newspaper or your missing leather belt lying on the little mattress. I never got around to putting it up into the attic. It's as if I knew that I wasn't finished with it yet. Altogether I feel as thrilled as if I'd just been shot in the head, or knocked off a sixty-foot pillar.

CHAPTER THREE

I spend a lot of time getting sick in the bathroom. I always wanted Robin to put in a second one downstairs. Now he realises that I was right. I can hear him banging at the door, but he'll have to wait.

'Angel,' he calls, 'are you OK?'

The green lino is hopelessly stained by the hair rinses I use. I have to use them, otherwise I'd be as grey as a badger, as grey as Nancy. When your head is hanging over a lavatory bowl early in the morning motherhood is not the wonderful experience it is reputed to be. If I puke once more my brains are going to shoot down my nostrils. That's how bad I feel.

'Angel?'

From where I crouch every man in the universe seems old and lecherous, with an evil stare in his eyes. Robin can wait. Two bathrooms. When I was expecting Anne and Ray and Jenny it was exactly the same. God help anyone who suffers from nausea. I'm afraid to come out of here in case I'm not finished throwing up. Robin will have to stand guard for a while longer. Jenny was born in January and all through the previous glorious summer things were exactly the same as now. Nancy came down and sat on the beach in Lahinch with us. There she talked about her own concerns while Anne and Ray whinged for minerals and chocolate, and the pain that was Jenny dug into my stomach. Lucky Nancy, never having to go on family holidays. Even in Lahinch that time she booked herself into the Aberdeen Arms while Robin and I roughed it with the kids in a caravan.

'Angel?' Robin hammers on the door.

There's no need to feel guilty when I can be as sick as this. It's punishment enough for any crime. It's like being at your own funeral and not quite dead. All that is required now is the eulogy. I'm only a trembling husk, hardly a human being at all.

If Robin had done as I suggested there would be another bathroom for him to use—and I don't feel like cooking food ever again after all this. As far as I'm concerned lunch will be a write-off, and everyone can go to a café. And what are you having, sir? Scallops in white wine? No—we'll try the omelettes instead. They are simpler to prepare. You can't have a baby without fertilising an egg.

I emerge wiping my mouth and Robin charges past me while Jenny rushes out of her room and nearly knocks me down. I realise that I'm not looking my best; even so, I'd appreciate a civil greeting accompanied by an apology. What I get is a grunt.

'Jenny!' I shout as she humps off down the stairs.

Naturally I made a mess of telling her about the expected baby—on her birthday too, trying to sweeten the news with large dollops of chocolate mousse. Well, I'm not thrilled about it either but what can I do?

Anne has offered to come back and stay in the house for the next few months. She is full of sympathy. She sees me as a martyr. 'I've talked it over with Brian. He'll understand if you want me back until it's over,' she said. I believe she means it. I couldn't bear it if she did come back. I don't want another fight. Forgive and forget and keep Brian outside the garden gate. 'How is Brian?' I hesitated before asking. I saw his wife and two children in the city centre the other day. 'Great.' A grin plastered itself across Anne's face.

I go through the motions.

I discover that Robin has left his pyjamas in a blue tangle on the floor. And I must rush, clean up, go shopping. I'd be glad if someone would give me a hand in the kitchen but Jenny has vamoosed. And I know it is January, but the heat in our kitchen is like winter in the tropics. I can feel the make-up melting off my face after five minutes. A second bathroom and a bigger kitchen without a range, that's what I should have.

'How do you feel now?' Robin asks.

He's immaculate—brown check suit with a thread of blue, blue shirt to match the thread, dark red tie with a small multicoloured, tear-shaped motif. No wonder he has done so well in business. Gallivanting off, all decked-up like that, every morning. As for me

—it's Robin's toast crusts and rasher rinds.

I'd like to go straight back to bed if you really want to know. Even a dirty saucer feels as heavy as lead.

I divert myself by trying to remember if Leo's nose is very hooked. It's like trying to remember a ghost—someone who is already in their tomb.

Now that Robin has gone off to work the only man around is the postman cycling up the garden path.

I'm the duchess type. So Leo told me.

I barely manage to finish off the kitchen, clear out the sitting room fireplace and make the beds before I must head off for the shops. My morning sequence is as crammed as a six-countries bus tour. And, except for the days that Betty comes, I'm driver and courier rolled into one.

There are certain things I skip—such as the cemeteries full of junk in Jenny's room.

Robin's dinner-jacket must be brought to the cleaners because whiskey was spilt on it at a stag dinner last week. Black velvet, with a red carnation like an ungranted wish withering in its buttonhole. It's the sort of jacket that I imagine John Keats would have fancied as he sat in his little brown house. I insisted that Robin buy it. He and I took a quick trip to Rome last October. We tried to visit Keats's house, but it was closed in protest about some atrocity or other. I can't remember what the actual cause was. All I remember is that we sat on the Spanish Steps surrounded by weirdos instead, and that while Robin tried to hold my hand I thought about Leo and felt stupidly pleased with myself.

I throw my umbrella into my car because this isn't Rome and that splashing water isn't the Trevi Fountain.

When we got back from Rome everything about Leo, even the back of his head, seemed different. But perhaps the change was in myself, I was filled with astonishing energy. Now the very thought of poking around the local shops is almost too much, the only thing that keeps me moving is the prospect of a lazy afternoon in front of the fire. Yes, I had astonishing energy when I got back from Rome—plus inventiveness. For instance, I made up all those crazy stories for May and Company about my fictitious friend called Noelle. Honestly, I should be considered for the Nobel Prize. Not that I'd be interested—all I want is a siesta in my armchair.

The one snag about Rome was that, according to my charts, it was the wrong time of the month for lovemaking. We refrained, even the night after that wonderful meal in the place with the fishing nets and the blue grotto. And then, as soon as we reached home, I submitted with a grim fatalism to Robin's embraces, for already the real situation had begun to dawn on me. 'I wish we could have done this in Rome,' Robin sighed. I remembered the fiasco of our honeymoon and felt that Rome had jinxed me twice.

But I won't dwell on it as I stand in the bacon shop waiting for the man with the shiny head to cut my rashers.

Doreen Barry is buying rashers as well. 'Streaky ones—much more economical, Angel,' she says, watching the pink and white meat curl, and twist, and fall from the slicer.

'Robin won't eat streaky. I have to buy him back.'

Doreen is coming from mass. I can see her prayerbook in her basket. She is a great one for religion—pounds to St Anthony, prayers for the holy souls. Prayers for Don all through November —the month for the dead—while the simplest supplications froze on my lips.

'Back are twice the price.' She shakes her head at my extravagance, and puts her own neat parcel in beside the prayerbook. 'How's everything?'

Doreen has a heavy hand with a powder puff. Her face looks pink and fuzzy. She is taller than I am, a fact I always find intimidating. Tall women remind me of Bel in her heyday, perched like a flamingo on her platform soles, ruling the roost in my father's house.

'Have you been to Dublin lately? Any news of your friend, Noelle?'

I don't trust myself to reply. Doreen has the gift of remembering pernickety details. Anyway, a sudden ache in the small of my back has made me faint-hearted. I don't want to discuss anything— Anne, Ray, Geraldine. I don't want her treating me as one of her sad cases. I have a sudden remembrance of Robin, ridiculously poignant in his red underpants, saying, 'I'll look after you, Angel, don't worry kiddo.' I'm overcome. I dash out into the street, beating a coward's retreat, forgetting the rashers.

I don't want my whole life broken up to be examined by the curious. It is my life, all I've got.

'Angel, this must make no difference to you and me,' that was one of the things Geraldine said in the aftermath. But sometimes people can't help changing, they can't keep the sharpening edge from their voices. They can't help evading each other's eyes when certain topics—trick-acting, manslaughter, tragic accidents, the dead boy's parents—are mentioned vaguely at social gatherings. 'I believe that they moved to a small house,' said a voice from a clutch of people crammed on the terrace at a midday cocktail party. A fat Welsh woman, drunk as a coot, fell down the steps and dislocated her knee. The conversation changed, but the arrow had pierced once more. 'What on earth would be the point of a big house when there are only two of us,' Geraldine said, and there was the sharpness again.

I sail down the street under the Switzer's umbrella which I bought in Grafton Street last August.

'You remind me of a ship in a bottle,' Leo said. 'Did you enjoy your lunch?' I couldn't even remember what we had eaten.

I start impulse buying. I buy some coffee beans in a smart shop. As soon as I get home, I'll float a few of them on the last of that Italian sambuca, and put my feet up and sip like a honeybee. Yes, I'll do a bit of lounging and lazing, spend my afternoon the way Robin's mother used to. I'll ensconce myself on our green sofa as comfortably as a plaster saint in a grotto, or my lady in her semi-detached castle while my lord sells insurance.

'I want to see the white woolly shawl in the window, please.'

'Shawl in the window?' The lazy girl behind the woolshop counter repeats my words and settles herself more comfortably on her stool.

'Yes.' I hide my impatience. 'I mean the openwork one, the white one, the one with the flower motif.' My head swims from trying to express myself clearly and patiently. But there is no need to get into a stew. Perhaps the girl isn't lazy, perhaps she is simply worn out from sitting up all night in a bed-sit crocheting these shawls. 'It looks handmade. It's beautiful.'

The girl yawns widely and I see how bad her teeth are. Which reminds me, I must make an appointment with my dentist. My teeth start to rot when I'm pregnant.

'That's a christening shawl,' the girl says, as if she's speaking to an idiot.

I change my mind. I absolutely forbid her to take it out of the window. I can see right away that it's too long, too square, too clumsy. Besides, this is a busy street and someone I know is sure to be passing by. I don't want the premature publicity, thanks. I'm sorry if I appear nihilistic, but the last thing I want in the world is another christening shawl. All I want is something to throw over my shoulders, like Robin's mother used to, during the long afternoons. There's no point in trying to persuade me. No point in shaking out the shawl for my benefit and saying, they're all the go with new mothers. I'm not a new mother and I have a christening shawl. It's as old as the hills but it will do.

I arrive home feeling ponderously insipid. I always thought that women in this kind of situation were tormented by agonies of conscience, driven to showy excesses of desperation. I just feel ridiculous. I sit in the front room, hunched over the fire which has not yet begun to throw off heat. I feel as if I have climbed a mountain. The rain has turned to sleet. I find myself looking at the clock so frequently that it is irritating. And then Jenny comes in from school. The new, sulky, silent Jenny who turns and walks out of the room the moment she spots me. She deliberately neglects to close the door.

'Jenny!'

I strain my ears for some response to my exasperated yell, but she has deliberately walked off, ignoring me as if I am nothing more than an overstuffed doll.

I complain about her later, as Robin and I drive out to Billy Black's party.

Billy Black's house is very hot in spite of the freezing winter, the central heating must be turned on full blast. It is almost hotter than the Via Veneto was last October. The house is quite a distance from the city, with—even in the dark—hints of a beautiful view.

'I suppose it is just a country cottage, really,' Phyllis Black suggests to her assembled visitors.

She is not serious. The only cottagey touch is the colour scheme—rich browns and blues, thickly flowered cretonnes, shiny dark wood. All the drinking glasses are Waterford crystal, the finest. Everything is five-star quality, Grade A.

I wouldn't be surprised if these taps in the bathroom proved to be solid gold—and the mouldings on the bathroom woodwork genuine gold leaf. Unfortunately I can't appreciate them fully as I'm getting sick again, very sick.

'Billy has told me your good news,' Phyllis whispers. She persists in being the perfect hostess even though it looks as if I have ruined her bathroom carpet. 'Of course it is we women who have to put up with the unpleasant side of it,' she soothes, dropping spotless cloths over the disgusting mess.

Even in the midst of my distress I have to admire her way with air freshener and disinfectant. Phyllis would never give in, I believe, if she found herself in my predicament. She unbolts the bathroom door and opens the window. The carpet is clean again, the air so sharp and purified it scrapes the lungs.

'You won't die this time,' she says gaily as she leads me back to the party.

I get a half-knowing look from one person and another.

CHAPTER FOUR

Robin and I have always enjoyed going to the pictures. In fact, a history of our joint relationship could almost be subtitled 'history of the cinema'. It began back in the Savoy of our home-town—an acid green building, square as a cell-block, with tip-up seats in the balcony, and hard chairs and wooden benches downstairs. Nowadays we belong to the city's film society.

The offering tonight is one of those dark blue German productions. It is a film about a foundling. Just watching the poor creature on the screen—incarcerated in a small dug-out on that peasant's land—exhausts me. There is nothing at all about his mother, not a clue. As far as I can make out he just dropped from the sky into the middle of this archaic set-up, was dumped on it, you might say.

Just as I was dumped on my father, who would probably have had a much better life if he hadn't had to rear me, if he hadn't had to take me by the hand and walk me down to mass on Sundays and holy-days while Bel lay in bed.

Some nineteenth-century philanthropists rescue our foundling, but as soon as he approaches some sort of normality the peasant comes back and kills him.

The Bells of St Mary's, *The Wizard of Oz*, *Rebecca*, *The Beast with Five Fingers*, *Stagecoach*, *The Young Lions*, *Waterloo Bridge*, these were some of the films that made a big impression on our growing-up. And of course the funnies, and *Gone with the Wind*. Scarlett O'Hara, with her, 'I'll think about it tomorrow.' (I have always been good at procrastination.)

I reach out for Robin's hand and squeeze it as the film ends with an autopsy and a close-up of the foundling's brain being dissected. Thanks a lot! I think I'll buy a video and rely on my own good taste.

Not that I haven't seen strange films in strange places. I once had a schoolfriend whose father was medical superintendent of a lunatic asylum. The remembrance pleases me, I can put it on ice and use it to embellish a Noelle story. I spent one mid-term break with this friend. Her family house was in the hospital grounds. We were allowed into the hospital's film shows. We sat alongside the inmates, who were all dressed in loose grey towelling wrappers, and who nodded and drooled over Nelson Eddie and Jeannette MacDonald in *Naughty Marietta* and other mild entertainments.

The film club seats are so uncomfortable that it's worse than sitting on rocks. It's a relief to stand up and shuffle out. What a life! Thank God we're not in the nineteenth century. I'm not going to have a foundling, I'm going to have a cherub. A tiny gilt cupid complete with bow and arrow, he glows inside me, warm as a torch. That doesn't mean that I'm released from my habitual search for a convenient lavatory bowl. Or that I'm spared the sight of myself, ashen and middle-aged, in the cloakroom mirror.

Robin and I arrive at the hotel bar holding hands. Holding hands is one of the odds and ends of romantic bliss that we've never discarded. I always watch elderly lovers with delighted admiration.

I have a memory of Mrs King, surprisingly active and busy once prised from her sofa, supervising a bathing party, and the way she helped Mr King, who had arthritis in his knees, to peel off his bathing trunks and replace them with heavy pale underpants. Their love seemed to be much more fitting than that of my father and Bel. As soon as I was old enough to understand, I used to lie awake waiting for the creak of Bel's door, the pattering steps on the landing, then the sounds from my father's room—Bel's laughter, his deep murmur—finally a silence which used to leave me sullen and lonely in the dark. I preferred the Kings, he standing and she kneeling in full view of where Robin and Nancy and I splashed in the river. 'It's not funny. You're not to look!' Nancy would scream furiously when Robin and I began to snigger.

'Two Paddies. One without ice,' Robin says to the barman. To me, 'A penny for them?'

Remember those sandy pools we fished in for hours? We never caught anything except pinkeens. 'Nothing.'

'How do you feel?'

'Everything's fine.' If it's a boy. 'I wouldn't mind having another boy.' My throat closes over the words as if I have tonsillitis.

Robin gulps the rest of his drink and stands up. 'Come on—this place is full of riff-raff.'

He drives the car home the way you'd take a jet plane down the runway.

That spring morning, almost a year ago now, I saw Nancy off on the ten o'clock train. She had been visiting us for a long weekend. I felt obliged to issue these invitations from time to time, just as she felt obliged to accept them. This visit hadn't been too bad. There had even been moments when we seemed to have the makings of a proper family party as we collected around the dining-room table. Although of course the very fact of eating in our dining-room made for a certain amount of claustrophobia and elbow-bumping. 'It's a shame you never had that silver teapot of Daddy's fixed,' Nancy said as she folded her linen napkin.

I threaded my way gaily across the grubby station tiles, and down the stone steps, into the weightless day. No more need for all the trimmings—best cutlery, best china. Even the fact that Robin had gone away for the day on business was a relief. The mood was light, the immediate outlook rosy. I even toyed with the idea of calling round to Geraldine's to tell her a titbit of bourgeois porn which concerned a couple we both knew. I hovered between certain pleasant possibilities before getting into the Fiat and driving straight home.

The police car outside our gate meant nothing to me. Of course it was an obstruction, I wasn't able to swing my own car into the driveway. It could wait. They were probably searching for television spongers in the house next door, I had paid our own licence myself. Or perhaps the old woman who lived by herself had been found dead, I hadn't noticed her peeping out of her window lately. That's the way my mind was working—in general terms of other people's troubles.

Our porch is like other porches along the road. You enter it from the side and have a view in through the sitting-room window as you do so. I could hear the telephone ringing in the hall. I don't know whether it was the insistent ringing or the shadowy figures in the sitting-room that struck me most forcibly as I pushed in my latchkey. They didn't seem to belong together, and they certainly didn't belong to Ray—who sprang through the hall into the porch to meet me.

He hopped about 'umming' and 'aahing' as I stood there smiling. Smiling and smiling like a fool. 'Auntie Nancy has gone,' I said. I didn't even bother to ask about the people inside, they could wait. 'I say, Ma, I've a bit of bad news,' and so on. At least Ray was wearing his shoes. Grubby runners, I'm afraid. I doubt if his paternal grandfather, Mr King, would have approved. But you must admit it's better than bare feet, especially out-of-doors. A guard came through the hall and said, 'Mrs King, I think you'd better step inside.'

'I forgot and pulled the trigger.' 'I forgot it was a gun.' 'I forgot where the trigger was.' Who cares what the exact words were in that cry that wriggled, ugly as a bulging vein, across the unblemished morning. The gun had been left in Geraldine's house for safe-keeping by one of Paul's clients because the pheasant-shooting season was over. 'I forgot it was Don.' Then there was nothing to prevent me from seeing clearly that the policemen were in our own sitting-room. It was the suddenness of it all that made me pummel Ray's T-shirt and shout, 'You stupid dope,' before brushing past him into the house.

A sudden blow—a heart attack, perforated ulcer, brain haemorrhage, the waiter knocking at our bedroom door in the *pensione* with news of my father's sudden death—you get a shock. When you recover you go back to beforehand and begin to rationalise your actions in a completely new light. O my God! If I had called in on Geraldine how would I have behaved? What could I have said? Perhaps my immediate reaction to the accident would have been to scream that it was an act of God, something He had been keeping in store for us until the time was ripe, a hairshirt which we all must wear. I could see in a flash that even I must be held responsible, I had been too pleasant, far too forgiving towards Robin and Geraldine.

Afterwards we clubbed together. There was no question of a

criminal charge, it was clearly an unfortunate accident. 'He didn't even move Don. He just waited right there for the ambulance man to come and carry him in,' Geraldine tossed me what crumbs she could.

I helped Geraldine to prepare the buffet supper for the mourners. Every so often my face cracked up and shiny streaks ran through my make-up. My hair dangled around my face. 'Of course you and Geraldine are close enough to be sisters. That makes it even more awkward for you,' May said. I was pleased when she dropped a forkful of coleslaw down the front of her pale linen dress.

Paul and Robin were both hunched and miserable, but Geraldine was magnificent. Really magnificent. Even the next day at the funeral mass, when we all went to pieces, and Ray cried so much that his jumper began to smell of wet wool, she was as cool as something that had stepped straight out of a polar cave, as shockingly bright and glittering as a perfect solitaire.

We arrive home and I'm still thinking about that miserable film, and the gruesome fate of the foundling. This is the last night I'll let Robin talk me into one of these depressing outings.

It is half past eleven but Anne is in our sitting-room. 'I still have my latchkey. I let myself in. I've been waiting for ages,' she says. She consults the man's gold watch, Brian's watch, which she is wearing. 'I told Brian I'd meet him at the corner at midnight.'

Robin and I keep our mouths shut. We vowed when Anne left that we'd let things run their course. It's her own funeral.

'I'm fascinated,' Leo said when I told him that Robin had banned Brian from our house, 'the Kings must thrive on drama.' 'He's a married man with two small children,' I said. I didn't tell him the rest of it—how Brian had had a row in public with his glamorous wife and picked her up and swung her round by her long fair hair.

But I think now that we should have made an altogether different arrangement, so many things have changed. If he lays a finger on Anne I'll wring his neck, although she doesn't look as if she is being abused.

'I didn't think you'd be going anywhere,' Anne says.

'Mama and I were at the pictures.'

I don't know when Robin started calling me Mama. It reminds me of my proper role. 'Hope everything is well with you and Dad.' Ray's most recent card from the kibbutz is on the mantelpiece, propped against the green marble souvenir of the Pope's visit, a statuette with, 'Young people of Ireland, I love you', inscribed on a silver disc.

'Ray seems to be getting on fine,' I say. I blink my eyes, trying to shake off the bad dream.

I took a taxi from the station to Stephen's Green and had my lunch in Bewley's. That's how I happened to buy a cherry log. The red lumps of fruit made me think of globules of blood. I handed over my coin to the lavatory attendant and went into one of the cubicles, but nothing doing. I was going to put the matter fair and square to Leo—and then what? Remind him of the cause, perhaps —the pair of us having crème de menthe *frappé* in the Stag's Head where my will turned as fragile as a twig in frost. 'Come on, Angel, let's get out of here.' My heart was forced into my mouth by the pressure of Leo's hand. I didn't care tuppence about subsequent events so why should he?

And why should I object to the way that another person—even if she is my daughter—conducts her life? Besides, she's older than Robin and I were when we got married.

Time passes. It's ten to twelve and I hear Jenny coming in the hall door, in spite of the fact that her absolute curfew time is eleven forty-five and she has school tomorrow.

She strolls into the room. 'I forgot,' that's all she has to say to her mother. Wide-eyed innocent Jenny, with 'I forgot', as if that is a perfectly logical answer.

'Don't give me that stupid excuse,' I say. 'Let me remind you of your last school report.'

'You're in great form,' she says rudely and walks past me, ignoring Anne and Robin, chewing some take-away concoction in a greasy container.

No wonder Jenny won't eat properly at mealtimes. No wonder she's yawning and grumpy and late for school most mornings.

'She's OK,' Anne intercedes.

'You're always criticising me,' Jenny grumbles.

That's very good. Break all the rules and then blame the person in authority. 'I hope you haven't been doing anything wild,' I say. I can't help glancing at Anne.

'It's time for me to go,' Anne says, looking at the tell-tale watch. And she's off, in full flight, crying over her shoulder, 'I said I'd be there dead on midnight.'

In the kitchen Jenny gives my inane attempt at a further rebuke the half-hearted shrug it deserves. I'm lucky to get even that much. I walk around the kitchen feeling like a giantess who has got lost in a Japanese garden. 'Pregnant' is all I can see in Jenny's eyes. My fat turnip feet can't make their way across these flimsy bridges. The assembled coffee ladies titter behind their fans as I stumble along the twisty paths. My shadow throws its huge dark patch over all the delicate blossoms.

Jenny crumples up the greasy container and throws into the sink. Then she lifts the lid of the bread-bin.

'What are you looking for?'

'Brown bread.'

I haven't baked brown bread for weeks, months, more than a year. Ray was the one who ate my brown bread. Rain begins to pelt against the window. Tomorrow is going to be a really dreadful day. Rain. Rain. A slice of supermarket swiss roll is the best I can offer. I have a memory of Ray eating brown bread smothered with honey as if that way he could sweeten his world again.

'Is Bel coming down to see us sometime?' Jenny asks.

'She wouldn't be able for it,' I say.

Jenny flits about like a restless moth. 'We didn't go up to visit her for ages,' she says.

No we didn't. The poor old golden cocker has had to sit by herself, looking through the bars of the gate. I've too many other things to think about.

There are clothes out on the line in that awful rain, and I hope that fellow turned up punctually for Anne.

Jenny is watching me with doubtful distaste, as if I'm Bette Davis in *All about Eve*. 'You're beginning to show already,' she says.

Sure, and my eyes are baggy and my jaw sags. So what—you can't be a skinny fifteen-year-old in tight trousers and a woolly jumper with brown leather elbow patches forever.

'Why doesn't someone bring Bel down in a car?' Jenny asks.

What's the point. Bel has gone ga-ga.

And I recognise that jumper. I remember sewing on those leather patches. 'What are you doing with Ray's pullover?' I scream.

The fridge shudders to off. White fridge. White-faced Jenny rubs her thighs nervously while she looks down at the poor pullover. She must have been in Ray's bedroom. No one is allowed to interfere with the things that he left behind, they must be kept safely for his return. In spite of my tiredness and pregnant condition I could demolish her with a good wallop.

'I'll put it back,' she mutters.

I could shoot her. Mustn't use that expression—there are so many words and thoughts that are becoming taboo. Oh Lord. Bel—the nuns do their best, she's OK. 'It was meant to be a joke,' Ray said. I hope it's true that you do not hear the shot that kills you. 'Give me that sweater and get on up to bed.'

Jenny's arms, when she peels off the garment, are pale and plucked as a chicken's wings.

'You're talking to yourself,' Robin points out when he comes into the kitchen a few minutes later.

I know what that's a sign of.

Chapter Five

My mind wanders in the direction of white weddings as Anne drives me up to the cottage. Wishful thinking.

'Here we are,' Anne's voice rouses me from my reverie. She looks like Alice in Wonderland as she parks Brian's car at the clearance opposite the cottage.

Rain pelts on the grass, the thickening hedges, and slants in the breeze across the lake. We hold newspapers over our heads as we scurry across the road, open the blue-painted iron gate, splash over the small patio with its ornamental urns.

'It's a suntrap in summer,' Anne says as she fiddles with the lock.

We step over the threshold and onto the red tiled floor. It's a dream cottage. We walk across the kitchen and Anne pushes open a door to reveal a sitting-room complete with deep armchairs. A silvery goatskin rug lies in front of a French stove.

'Isn't it cosy?' she says.

The stove has been lit. The room is warm. Rain, licking against the windowpanes, blurs the view of the hills on the opposite side of the lake.

'What do you think?' Anne asks.

Brian has certainly looked after things, although how long the arrangement will last I cannot say. I am publicly aiding and abetting a sorry state of affairs by being here, that's what I think. 'You could be anywhere,' I say to Anne.

The cottage is half-an-hour's journey from Limerick city. Brian bought it as a weekend retreat, according to Anne. Now he and she are using it as a base because Brian's wife has been given his family house. Dublin, Limerick, Leo's central city mews, Brian's lakeside cottage—these places are all traps.

'You know what I think,' I say. 'I think you should be going out with somebody you can marry.'

'Oh, Mama, leave the Girl Guides for Aunt Nancy,' she says.

That's another of Nancy's roles. Guider King—blue beret, brown belt, polished buckle, shiny brogues. Nancy—wait until she hears I'm pregnant. She'll accuse me of trying to ruin Robin. She accused me of ruining Anne by treating her affair with Brian so indulgently. 'It's time you woke up,' she said, when she heard the news that Anne was allowed to come home and visit us. Or else she'll say something consoling like, 'Oh, my God—at your age! The child will be retarded.' That's my sister-in-law, just the person to cheer you up.

I'm nervous and anxious. I'm sorry now that I agreed to let Anne bring me up here. I want us to have our coffee and biscuits and get away again as quickly as we can. 'I brought some shortbread,' I say, taking the packet out of my bag.

I won't even take my coat off although the thick wool sleeves hamper my movements as I sip my coffee. When I reach for a biscuit I topple my mug and a dark stain spreads over the purple tweed upholstery. I can hear Brian's cry of anger when he comes in and sees what I have done to his good chair. And the earthenware mug splinters into fragments on the red tiles. Well, it was Anne's idea that I come and look at where she is living. I was brought here much against my will. My eyes smart. Any enthusiasm I felt for the cottage dies away.

I look out of the window at the grey sky, and the clouds racing along the tops of the hills, while Anne takes care of the breakage.

I'm always doing awkward things nowadays. I long to, but I won't say anything. I won't even ask again about plans, even though, as Anne works in Brian's office, she will be *sans* job as well as *sans* boyfriend if the affair breaks up. I'll keep my mouth shut. There are enough harpies in the world.

'No man will want her afterwards,' Nancy said. 'I'm only saying to your face what everyone else will say behind your back.' She persisted in the same strain long after I had told her to stop being bad-minded.

I watch as a tall girl wearing red woolly stockings comes dashing in from the road. She stops and peers through the kitchen window and then raps sharply on the front door. Her hair is fashionably cropped. Anne runs out and there is much talk, laughter, exclamations. The red-stockinged girl is called Bridget. She is just thrilled to find Anne at home.

'The cottage is simply super, Anne. It's a dream. And look at the view, and the fantastic patio.'

'It's a suntrap in summer,' Anne recites like a parrot.

Where did the gorgeous Welsh dresser come from? If Bridget lived here the first thing she would buy is a budgie. Honest. It's all that it needs to make it absolutely divine—doesn't Anne think so? And look at that fabulous rug! She bets that Anne lies down on it to do her Jane Fonda work-outs. Bridget flits from item to item, reiterating her envious admiration. 'What wouldn't I give!—There's no doubt about it—some people people have all the luck . . . Isn't it ideal!' There is no discouraging her. 'What do you think, Mrs King? Isn't it fabulous?—How about upstairs, Anne? The view from the bedroom must be brilliant.' Anne and I remain in the kitchen while Bridget clatters up the narrow wooden stairs and down again with the purposeful energy of a cannonball. 'And— wowee—that bed. Talk about dark horses. I only heard about yourself and Brian out at Durty Nelly's the other night when the gang were there. Of course, I always told you he was cracked about you,' she says.

She was on her way to visit an uncle ('An ancient warrior type. You've no idea. Still thinks it's nineteen-sixteen. But bags of cash. A fabulous character . . .') when she spotted Brian's car outside the gate.

A bold girl. That would be Nancy's assessment of Bridget. A bold girl who is too free with her tongue. Even so I think it would be easy to be courageous with a friend like Bridget backing you up.

Almost as good as having a husband like Robin. I'm lucky. Robin is wonderful. Nothing can go wrong. We have always stuck together.

'I'm just baffled,' I say when Bridget has left us to continue her journey to the village. The sky has lightened with her departure and is showing sunset shades of lemon and pink. I want Anne to drive me home before it gets dark.

'Oh, Bridget is a scream,' Anne says.

It's not just Bridget that I find remarkable.

'That's because you grew up in a different world,' Anne says.

I find that I'm grinning. I cannot help thinking fondly of Leo and last September. I'm feeling much better these days. The nausea stage is over, I haven't vomited for over a week. Yes, Leo is bathed in the same happy light as the glowing sky. 'I'm glad I've seen this place after all,' I say. 'Now I won't worry so much.'

Anne sparkles. 'Hang on a tick,' she says. 'I want to change my clothes.' She is meeting Brian in town and they are going to the pictures.

I wait in the sitting-room, memorising its details—the stone owl in the window, an old theatre poster, a patchwork cushion. Then I feel that they look like things a woman would choose, and that probably Brian's lawful wife put them there. I rub at the place where I spilt coffee, but it remains as an unwanted souvenir. There is a pair of men's sandals beside the bookshelf. I go over and study the titles. Gardening, fly fishing, some spy thrillers, a political directory. On the top shelf a sheet of paper is curled into a roll. I can't help myself. It is one of those mock newspapers on which you can insert a headline concerning someone you know. I uncurl it delicately to read the caption. BRIAN CLARKE LOSES WIFE IN CARD GAME.

Anne has frizzed out her hair and is wearing a flouncy dress from an Indian shop under a tweed coat.

'Do I look alright?' she asks before tying her belt.

Anyone with a waistline like Anne's has to look terrific. 'Beautiful, and as thin as a whip,' I say.

'You know, Mama—you needn't speculate about that side of things. I'm not going to get pregnant.' She jangles the car keys. 'I'm taking care of things. Of course I intend to have one someday. I want to find out what it's like.' Then she gets flustered, 'Not that I don't think you're wonderful—you and Daddy.'

'Come on,' I say quickly, 'I want to get home.'

Anne and I don't speak much as we drive down the road. I'm thinking about birth-control. Leo and I never discussed it although the subject has preoccupied me during most of my married life.

I can remember the day that *Humanae Vitae* was published.
Jenny was just a baby. We had made up our minds that we didn't
want any more kids. In fact I was on the pill. We were in Kilkee
on our holidays. 'I can sympathise with you and May, but in our
case it's a question of wanting more and not having them. Only
children are a bad idea,' Geraldine said to me. The day after
Humanae Vitae was published Robin drove up to Limerick to
collect my next month's quota of pills. A long way away, and a
long time ago. Jesus! I feel ancient.

The weather was glorious—an idyll of sun, sea and swimming.
Robin and I made love in the bed with the lumpy mattress almost
every night. It was only when we came home that things became
less harmonious. Robin spent a great deal of time reading the letters
to the paper about the Pope's pronouncement that all forms of birth
control were banned. I was too busy coping with Jenny to pay
much attention. It was only when he brought me home a large
manilla envelope bulging with literature about natural birth-control
and the Billings method that I discovered how seriously he was
taking the matter. He had gone to several priests. 'They all say the
same thing. It's a mortal sin,' he announced. Jenny was upstairs
wailing in her cot. 'You must be joking,' I said to Robin. But he
wasn't—a long way away, and a long time ago.

And now—at forty-two years of age, after all my trouble, what
a mess.

'There's always a risk,' that's what Billy Black said in the winter
of 1968 when I asked him to explain the Billings method in more
detail. 'There's always a risk, Angel. You've got to be sensible about
it, don't take chances in the middle of the month. That's what it's all
about. You'll be fine. You and Robin can relax and enjoy yourselves
tonight.' He patted me on the back, then watched me bump the pram
down his front steps and start the long trudge home.

'What I really need is a car for myself,' I said to Robin that night.
It was after midnight. We had just had sex. My throat was burning
from too much gin and my body felt like pulp. 'I'll buy you
anything you want. You know that,' Robin said. He reached for
my hand. 'Are you OK?' he whispered. I was too tired to reply.

I passed my driving test a few months later. Even so, I never drive long distances. Up and down to Dublin on the train, inventing new excuses.

I remember that the Pope got criticism from many sources, some of them very reliable. 'Dear Father,' I wrote to one of them, 'I would like you to know how much I appreciate your stand . . .' 'Dear Mrs King, It is because of women in your position . . .' he replied.

Edna and her family were also in Kilkee during the *Humanae Vitae* business. She persuaded some of the wives to meet in the Victoria Hotel. The few of us who turned up talked and talked until we got so discouraged about being women that we went into the sing-song in the bar. 'Albert and I always give up sex for Lent,' May told us. The chief thing, as far as all of us were concerned, was to obey the rules laid down by the priest. The word 'orgasm' was never mentioned, although one woman did volunteer that she had been asked in confession if there had been any loss of spermatozoa on her husband's part. The spermatozoa were what mattered, not the feeling of delight between her legs.

'Don't bother me with that rubbish,' Geraldine said when I relayed the gist of our discussions. 'As I can't get pregnant, I don't see how it concerns me,' and she stretched herself out on her sunbathing mat.

Damn!

'Fools rush in,' I said, unbuttoning my coat before Leo had even put his latchkey into the lock of the mews house. He waited, watching me, while I walked around the dim quiet interior, making complimentary remarks. All the time I knew that I didn't want to be there. When I eventually stopped and stood aimlessly beside the drawn curtains Leo said, 'I could fall for you in a big way.' The curtains were yellow and white—papal colours. I felt that we should pull them back and let the outside world see in. 'Have you changed your mind?' he asked when I hesitated beside the big bed with its satin eiderdown. I looked at him quickly. He seemed cold, dry, and unenthusiastic. I felt that he had suddenly lost interest in me. It was humiliating. 'No', I said, but my voice was so shaky that I couldn't say anything more. I began to unfasten my dress. 'We don't have to,' Leo said.

It seemed a million years ago since Robin had said the same thing as he stared at me in a Roman bedroom. In those days everything was very strict—because of the fasting laws of the time we were starving when we got to our wedding meal, by bedtime I had indigestion as well as my period.

I turned to Leo and said, 'What do you think?' I thought I would probably have hysterics if, after all my trouble, we didn't end up in bed together. Leo slipped his hand inside my bodice and rested it against my pounding heart. As he drew me towards him I thought I was going to collapse.

'Damn, damn, damn!!! We've got a puncture,' Anne says as the car swerves in against the grass embankment.

I have never had the energy to learn anything about cars except how to drive them. In fact, offhand I don't even know what make Brian's car is. It is silvery grey and has blue upholstery with headrests and the radio sounds better than the one in Robin's car. That's all I know about it.

'A whistling woman and a crowing hen—two unlucky things to have around a house,' my father used to say. I never whistle, and I have never attempted to change a wheel. I think we should flag someone down and get a lift into the city as fast as we can.

'And leave the car abandoned by the side of the road! That's crazy,' Anne says. She pulls some tools out of the boot in a convincing way.

It is raining again. I have no choice but to climb out reluctantly and stand beside her holding a torch. It takes ages. I give up counting the cars that whizz past when I reach one hundred. My feet are soaking and a thick dank smell rises from the earth. And I need to pee so badly that my knickers are unpleasantly damp when at last we bundle back into the car. The hem of Anne's dress is dangling limply below the hem of her coat. She looks a fright.

'I don't care so long as I have the wheel fixed,' she says in her contrariest manner.

I feel sure that she has put on the spare wheel incorrectly, in fact I am certain that the car has developed a dangerous wobble. I become convinced that we are going to be killed before we reach Castletroy.

Well, that's one way of having my problems solved.

CHAPTER SIX

Blood pressure OK, heart fine, ankles hardly swollen at all. This morning Billy Black was as proud of me as if I'd just passed my driving test first go. I could run a mini-marathon, play a game of tennis, go on a ten-mile hike. That's what he thought.

I'm in terrible shape. That's what I thought.

Even so, I've come up to visit Bel. On the phone the nuns were inclined to apologise—as well they might. They thought Bel's condition—that perhaps—in the circumstances—I'd like to see her. By the time we arrived things had improved so now it's just a routine visit. Nothing to get excited about, nothing to make my heart thump.

'She'll be delighted to see you. You'll have lots to talk about,' says the young nun with the black, bad-tempered eyebrows. She leaves us with Bel in a spare, monotonous room.

'We were just passing by and thought we'd call in,' I say loudly. She's very frail, looking at her in the bed, I can see that. 'You're in the right place. It's no weather for sitting out in your chair,' I say heartily.

'She's as bright as a button,' the passing ward-sister tells us, studying a long sheet of paper with half-closed eyes.

I suppose they have so many old parties lying comatose in these places that any who respond to attention with even a twitch qualify as alert.

Bel looks like some old biddy who has just been fed a half-pint of gin. Though we can see from the tray on the bed-table that it was something in gravy with mashed potatoes and turnips. Very good too, judging by the cleanly-scraped plate belonging to the patient in the next bed.

'Why don't you eat up your lovely dinner?' I ask.

'I'm counting on you to help me through this,' I said to Robin as we climbed the stairs. But he's no help at all. He sits on the opposite side of Bel's bed, looking at me as if he thinks my mind has blown.

Bel's eyes are so blank she could be blind. She isn't in a bed, she's in a cot. It has steel railings to keep her from falling out, just like an infant. I suppose they pull them right up during the night.

Have mercy on me. We'll have to get a cot. I gave our old one to May, years ago. She wanted it for their summer lodge in Kilkee. It must be in bits by now.

Robin's silence, combined with Bel's, is too much. I begin to talk incessantly to cover up the lack of sociability. Talk, talk— otherwise my eyes will start to swim. What am I talking about? God knows. Just futile sentences flying from my lips.

Here comes a tea tray to replace the dinner tray. We must have been here for hours—but we haven't, it only feels that way. And look at the tea tray, everything you could want—chips with the sausages, ketchup on a saucer. 'Why don't you try some of your lovely tea, Bel?' I take one of the smaller chips, dip it in the ketchup and tip it against Bel's mouth. I've done this before—held a lolling head steady, taught someone to eat.

The room clatters with cutlery.

'Come on, Bel. Everyone else is enjoying theirs.' You wouldn't get better in any hotel.

It's not fair, my grey wool coat, my only loose coat, is showered with ketchup. Honestly, I think people who bring elderly relatives or invalids to live with them deserve to be canonised. But Bel was always difficult. I remember her getting out of the dentist's chair years ago, and marching home with her mouth all frozen up because she'd changed her mind about getting a tooth out. She put up with the neuralgia afterwards rather than pocket her pride and go back. She can put up with being hungry now. I should have known better than to try coaxing her. She's not a baby, she's an ailing old woman.

Robin and I quarrel about Bel and my coat and the ketchup as we drive home.

'It was an accident. Bel couldn't help it. What do you expect when you ram your fingers down her throat? She probably thought that you were trying to choke her,' he says.

'I wish I had choked her,' I say. I have a vivid sensation in which my fingers are tightening on Bel's windpipe. All I need now to turn me into a murderess is for Robin to start telling me that Bel was as good as a mother to me.

Instead he says something worse, he says, 'Your father's old girlfriend deserves better than that.'

My father was too decent to give Bel the brush off, that's why I'm stuck with her now. 'What do you mean?' I challenge instead.

'I don't mean anything. I'm just stating a fact.'

I try to concentrate on the passing landscape, but it is too dark to see very much. I can even smell the blasted ketchup on my coat. The car heater is on and so my feet have begun to swell.

Robin reaches out and pats my knee. 'Be realistic—lots of men have girlfriends, so why not your daddy?'

His gesture and remark just make me feel more perverse. 'No they don't. And if they do it's a mortal sin,' I counter. Then I press my lips tightly together so that I won't say anything more.

Visiting Bel always has a bad effect on me. She stirs my consciousness like a dirty word, a dirty smell. Her image has hovered over my most intimate moments and brought them bad luck. If it wasn't for Robin I would never go near her. I should never have married, never borne children. I should have bought myself a vibrator and lived like a recluse.

Edna bought herself a vibrator recently, while she was in London on a shopping trip. She dropped this titbit of information into a pool of Saturday evening hotel-lounge natter. 'What do you mean, a vibrator?' It was Doreen Barry who asked. 'Noelle tells me they're wonderful. She brings one everywhere,' I chipped in. There was a sense of unease, of wives looking over their shoulders to make sure that the men were all up at the counter. Edna smirked across. 'Good for Noelle,' she said.

Noelle, Noelle—where did I dig you out of? What am I going to do with you now? 'I heard from Noelle the other day. Her father is dying—cancer of the liver or something like that.' I speak in a brisk tone to Robin, raising my voice above the noise of the engine.

'Everyone has it,' Robin answers just as non-committally.

'Noelle says he is just skin and bone.' I continue to spin something out of nothing—a web to conceal myself.

Robin was pleased when I told him my fairy-tale about bumping into a woman whom I had known as a girl in school, and that I had arranged to meet her again. Noelle, a new word, a new concept, a touchstone, something we could refer to without doing each other damage. She was a point of contact, a spotlight in the dark. I was dazzled by my own success. Once I even went so far as to announce, 'Of course I have really found myself a sugar-daddy,' when I had supposedly been scouring Dublin antique shops with Noelle for a particular type of oil lamp, but had in fact been eating *bliny* with Leo in a Russian restaurant. What a mess!

Noelle—I offer you now as an awkward apology, there is no point in acting sore.

We arrive in the city and, instead of driving home, go to a restaurant and order steaks. The owner takes my coat and hangs it on the coat-stand. I feel enormous, blown up from travelling. Robin reaches across the table and presses my hand. I begin to feel wanton. I want to make love. My palms tingle so much with desire that I find it difficult to hold my knife and fork. My knee, when it brushes against Robin's trouser-leg feels like a hyacinth bulb that is ready to flower. My gestures become so clumsy that I send my wineglass flying onto the floor. I remember a corny old joke about a man coupling with his wife in a restaurant, after the asparagus, but the words elude me. How awful it would be if Robin ditched me. Tears are beginning to run down my cheeks.

'Perhaps your wife wants to lie down,' the manager is saying.

To lie down would be paradise, but Robin disagrees. He is going to take me home. We should have gone there in the first place, he says, not, of course, that I'm drunk. It was the heat of the restaurant after the heat of the car.

'I want you,' I find myself saying on the way home. 'I want you.'

'Take it easy,' he replies, 'take it easy.'

The mink coat knocks me sideways. And I have a mink jacket already, not full length, it's true, but perfectly wearable.

Unfortunately, because of my increased bulk, the coat makes me look like a dealer in antiques—one of those women you see at auctions, pulling faces over hairline cracks in someone else's most treasured possessions. All I need are a pair of blue-rimmed bifocals hanging from a gold chain.

I sit on our green velvet sofa, wrapped in the coat's voluminous folds and say, 'Robin, you shouldn't have.' And I've nothing to wear under it except an old black grow-bag. All my good dresses are pushed to the back of the wardrobe. My legs buckle if I get into high-heels.

Robin smiles. Butter wouldn't melt in his mouth. 'I hoped it would fit and it does. You look grand.'

If it was left to me I wouldn't give you two pounds for this coat.

'You look ready for breakfast at Tiffany's,' Robin says admiringly.

I feel like the morning-after. 'I'd rather have used the money to buy new curtains for this room,' I say. (Or a plane ticket for Israel so that I could fly out and visit Ray.) I don't want to look grand. I want to be thin again and have only three children—Anne, Ray and Jenny. But protestations sound feeble and Robin doesn't take them seriously. I hitch the garment higher over my tummy.

'Wear that the next time you go out with the ladies,' Robin says.

It's as heavy as the wages of sin. It will certainly hit the local headlines. 'It makes me feel like a fallen woman,' I say. It makes me feel as brittle as a cut-crystal bird. It makes me want to go out and get drunk. When Robin comes and strokes my furry back it makes me want to howl like a forsaken bitch.

'You're no fallen woman, and we'll get new curtains as well,' Robin says.

It's the game of Happy Families and he holds all the winning cards.

By evening I feel like early to bed, and even Robin must admit that with the coat on I'm so bulky that I can hardly get into the car. We are going to a meeting. Some people debating the question of abortion. Feelings are high because it has become a political issue.

I find I need the coat because the hall is cold. There is an odd variety of chairs. The one thing that they have in common is that they are all uncomfortably small. I wish I'd stayed at home, watched TV and had a few drinks. The speakers spend most of their time getting tangled up in the microphones. When they're not extricating themselves from a microphone flex, they shuffle through messy bundles of paper.

'Bring in abortion and next thing we'll have euthanasia,' one of them brays.

He makes me think of Bel wasting away.

The chair Robin eventually finds for me seems to have belonged to a cinema or theatre in better days. It comes complete with built-in ashtray.

'These things must be exposed before it's too late,' a thin unhealthy looking man says earnestly.

When the nurses pull back Bel's bed-coverings there must be nothing except a sour-smelling puddle between the pasty face and the withered toes.

It's a strange world. A thin woman, dressed in a mixture of red-and-white gingham and green wool, pins a picture of something—I suppose it's a foetus—on a blackboard. I'm more interested in euthanasia. For myself, I'd rather be put peacefully to sleep forever than turn into a living tomb.

I know a lot of people in the audience. The couple from next door, May and her husband and two of their sons, sleepy looking youths in neat sports jackets. Ray never palled around with either of them. May is shaking her head and frowning in my direction.

Robin whispers anxiously, 'Do you want to leave?'

No. It's too awkward.

CHAPTER SEVEN

Today I feel that things are going from bad to impossible. In the first place we should never have come up to Killaloe. It is too near the cottage where Anne is. I haven't told Robin about my short excursion into enemy territory.

There are two roads that lead from Limerick to Killaloe. I suppose it was mutual consent that made us take the twisty one, the one that doesn't pass the cottage gate.

The very first people we meet are May and Albert. We have just been down to look at the cabin cruisers. On the way back there they are, toiling up the slope.

May says, 'I heard your news, Angel. I lit a candle for you at mass this morning.'

Irritating tears gather behind my eyes. I have trouble holding them back. Robin and I drove up after Sunday lunch in the hope that we might find some green promise of spring. Now any chance of a pleasurable afternoon is extinguished. We must stagger on through the rest of it with May and Albert, the invalid, for company. It's not my idea of a great afternoon.

It is May who takes charge, leads the conversation. She is against drugs, beards, bishops on television, and all political parties. 'Our politicians are nothing but a crowd of billy-goats—'

'Why don't you put yourself up for election so?' Robin interrupts her rudely. She is having her usual effect on him. She is putting him in a bad temper.

'I will. I will,' May says.

You must admire her guts and endurance. Things must be difficult since Albert had his stroke, but she doesn't complain.

She and Robin start arguing so vehemently that they move on ahead while I'm kept busy seeing that Albert doesn't fall over a loose stone or into a pothole. His speech is greatly improved. Last year it came out in a series of stifled yelps. Today I can catch most of his words. 'Thank you . . . Ver' col'.' However, his walk is still shaky. I keep thinking he is going to topple over, but each time he manages to right himself just as I am reaching out to grab him. He reminds me of those weighted toys that bob up smiling every time you remove your pressing hand.

I feel guilty about Albert. He travelled down on the same evening train as I did on one of my Dublin-and-back excursions last autumn. I got up quickly from my seat as soon as I saw his loose, jiggling frame being helped into the carriage by the social worker that May had inveigled into travelling with him on his trips to a Dublin speech therapist. But it was too late. I knew that Albert was watching me as I sneaked my way into the next compartment. I'm sure he felt snubbed. Nothing can be done about such lapses of behaviour. I hope Albert thought I had seen someone else I was supposed to meet further down the train. I hope he understood that I didn't want to push myself in on top of his misfortune. I'd hate him to think it was lack of sympathy.

We walk very, very slowly along the last uphill stretch between the trees. May and Robin are way ahead of us. The path grows dark and narrow as an alleyway. I allow Albert to clutch my arm more tightly for the final bit. I think it's unfair of May and Robin to leave us so far behind.

Poor Albert, I send him a sidelong glance. 'You're looking fine,' I say with well-wishing heartiness.

He stops dead in his tracks, disentangles his arm from mine, and looks at me dully. I'm wearing my mink coat again—for Robin's sake. It's too heavy, so I open the buttons.

'Like,' Albert says.

I hear the word clearly—'like'. His hand reaches out as suddenly as a bat from under a slate and flies straight to its target. His fingers tremble so hard against my stomach that I imagine May and Robin must hear the rustles, but they have moved on out of sight.

When Albert smiles a dribble trickles from the corners of his mouth. 'Nice,' he says. 'Nice.'

I feel terribly sorry for him. And glad that he's not bigger and stronger than I am. Because this is probably how a lot of women get themselves raped. By sauntering along carelessly, thinking that they're doing the world a good turn.

'Please. I'm pregnant,' I say carefully. 'That's why I'm so nice and fat.'

'Preg . . .' he says. 'Preg . . . g . . . g.' He gives up.

And he must know already. May knows. The whole town knows.

Happily Albert's hands have returned to their proper place because Robin is coming down through the shrubs. He's shouting at us to get a move on. The hotel bar is open. We'll go in and have a drink. Albert shakes himself, taps his walking stick against the ground and crawls upward, ignoring my proffered arm.

'He likes to do it by himself,' May calls bossily.

She came back, not because of Albert, but because of me, I might have slipped or something.

'You're not used to him,' she says when I get close to where she stands beside the laurel bushes.

Am I glad!

The hotel lounge is as miserable as most of these places are out-of-season, when not much is happening. I sit beside Robin and feel a complete ass as I avoid Albert's eye. The only other customer is a young man in shabby bell-bottoms. To keep out the draught, a piece of brown cardboard has been stuck across the door to the sun-terrace. It has as much atmosphere as a turf shed.

'Someone paid a nice pile of money for that beautiful mink coat,' May says, adopting her interviewer's manner.

'Robin did. It was a surprise present,' I say stupidly.

May claps her hands. 'A surprise! Was it because of the baby?'

'Yes.'

Robin is staring so intently at the view of the lake that I know he is furious.

May says, 'You're going to find this new child very difficult. I'd need to do a training course myself before I could handle a baby. I'm a wreck after a few hours with Francesca's tot.'

I look out of the window, we all look out of the window, as several more cars pull up outside. Their doors open. A good crowd of people struggle out onto the tarmacadam. Young men and women and several small children. There is a certain amount of confusion—shouting, laughing, slapping, whinging, the unloading of baby buggies. They all come trooping into the bar. The place turns into a bear-garden. It is as noisy as an All-Ireland Football Final.

'Isn't that beautiful! And you're facing into it all again, Angel.' May presses her hands to her ears and looks at the rowdy young women in their tight jeans and shiny blouses, balancing babies on their hips and sipping vodka and tonics. 'I bet Jenny's not too pleased about the news,' she says.

Albert begins to make cryptic noises. A word comes out, 'Want.' He is nodding energetically at Robin.

'Of course we want it,' Robin says.

Albert continues to nod in vigorous assent. 'Angel ... is ... lovely.' He says the sentence clearly.

I huddle in my mink coat as furtively as a double-dealing street Arab. I'm going to get an unbelievably bad attack of the jitters.

May is peeved. 'I think that when a woman gets to forty she should stop having children.'

'Angel and I ...' Robin begins, then changes his mind.

I leave them to muddle along and look out at the cars, at the people in the distance walking across the bridge. I wish I was any place but where I am.

At least I'm healthy. Billy Black will tell you that, and if I keep my mouth shut no one will get hurt.

May asks me if I have chosen a name for the baby. 'Moses!' I say.

The young mothers in their smock blouses jabber away at the counter.

'Moses!' May repeats. 'Has there been any news of Ray lately? How is he getting along in that colony ... or whatever it is?' She makes no attempt to veil her curiosity.

Robin looks as pained as if someone had dropped a lump of iron on his toe.

'Moses is quite a usual name in Israel,' I say. And a happy New Year to you too!

I excuse myself and go to the cloakroom with the silhouette of the crinoline lady on the door. One of the young mums is in there with her child. A stripy muffler is wound several times over her huge polo-neck jumper and yet she still looks skinny. She wears no make-up, steel-rimmed glasses, and her hair is cropped as short as the little boy's who is using the lavatory. She looks as if she probably knows everything there is to know about independence and self-help. She looks a thousand years younger than I do.

'It is chilly in here,' she says, as if passing some sort of comment on my mink.

'I think it is going to rain,' I answer.

I don't even need to use the lavatory. I see her watching me suspiciously as I stand there fiddling with my hair.

I know as soon as I get back to the lounge that something has happened. Even May looks as if she has lost her tongue. Then I see Brian and Anne at the counter. They must have arrived while I was in the cloakroom. I can see by the hurt look Anne sends in our direction that she has already attempted a greeting and been ignored. It is too late to do anything about it now. You're on your own, kiddo. Robin sits with sunken head, watching his pint. I see the expression on Brian's face too, the darkening anger. I sketch a wave but he yanks Anne from her stool and the two of them walk out in spite of the fact that the barman has their drinks ready.

What a day. 'What a debacle!' as Robin's mother used to say, tearing up the bookmaker's dockets and mournfully putting the shreds into a paper bag after she had listened to the English racing results on the wireless and found that all her horses were down the field again.

I was right about one thing, it has started to rain. Robin and I get soaked walking back to our car, which is quite a distance from the hotel. It is our own fault. We were the ones who elected to stay behind and have one last drink on our own instead of allowing May to drive us to our car. So she departed in a gyration of admonishments. 'Don't overdo it, Angel . . . Remember your age . . . As for you, you bad boy . . . What we women have to put up with!' To which Robin muttered, 'Kiss my arse,' while I pretended not to notice Albert's hand on my knee as he struggled to stand up.

All we need to complete the fiasco is the two of us splashing down the road, me in my mink, and the drink we didn't want sticking in our gullets while water runs down our foreheads in rivulets.

'Just one request,' Robin says as he unlocks the car, 'don't inflict May on me again.'

You're lucky it wasn't Albert, I think.

Neither of us mentions Anne and Brian.

I'm in such a contrary mood that I pretend there is nothing to eat in the house. All I want is to be left alone to recover myself. I wish I was a nun. Thank goodness the fridge is empty and Jenny is out. Luckily I'm not hungry. Robin can make himself a slice of toast if he wants to, or go back out to that hotel, or to a hotel in the city, and see if he can get a steak or a mixed grill. As for me, I'm just going to sit quietly and read a book. I pull the vegetable rack out from under the kitchen sink because I know it contains nothing but a few small squashed onions and shrivelled potatoes.

'There's a packet of fish fingers,' I weakly suggest. I know he loathes fish fingers.

'Can't we both go up the road and have something?' he ventures.

I refuse and, with a fine show of reasonableness, go into the front room and settle myself with a book. Fortunately the central heating is on and Jenny lit the fire.

'We might meet somebody,' Robin says.

I shake my head. I'm nearly dead from meeting people. I'd like to tell him how Albert behaved when he and I were left behind on the footpath today. I'd like to ring up May and discuss it and hear her vociferous dismay. It is only seven o'clock, I couldn't bear to go out again and sit around until ten-thirty or so, being chatted up by some casual neighbour. I'd rather curl up, like the cat, beside the fire. Or perhaps I'll have a very early night. A few pages of my book after Robin leaves, then there is just enough cold meat to make a sandwich, and bed before nine.

'Cheer up,' Robin says.

'All I need now is word that your sister is planning another visit,' I say.

Dragging in Nancy's name is inexcusable. Robin's face falls. Any aspersions on his family upset him.

I wouldn't go out again if you paid me. I take pleasure in dashing any faint hopes Robin might have.

And yet, when he has gone I'm restless, uneasily aware that the evening has become a void. Was this what I wanted? To be left alone in the darkness. The silence quickly becomes oppressive. Where is everyone? Where is Jenny? I don't want another drink. Even so, I take a bottle of Pernod from the drinks cupboard. Robin and I bought the bottle in Paris some time ago. We hardly ever use it.

The aniseed taste reactivates a memory of a meal eaten *tête-à-tête* in a restaurant. The place was popular and crowded. Looking around, we could spot only one other diner who was definitely older than we were. 'We're becoming *les anciens*,' I said to Robin. Yet I wasn't even forty then, pre-Leo, pre-kibbutz, pre-this, pre-big row about Robin and Geraldine. Shall I continue?

It was Paul, in fact, who made all the fuss, roaring and ranting up and down the town until it looked as if some unholy gang-bang had taken place. It was Paul who couldn't be induced to let the matter drop, who swore that the culprits should pay for their folly. It became a moral necessity, pleading was useless against his cracked logic. Either he must leave or else Geraldine, preferably all four of us should split and head for the four points of the compass. 'But what about the house?' Geraldine asked. They had just laid a new carpet in the hall, new ceramic tiles in the kitchen. They were planning to install a bathroom suite with gilded dolphin taps. 'If you choose to stay you can, I'd rather live in a cubbyhole,' Paul hissed with single-minded bitterness.

'It was only once or twice,' Geraldine said to me. I was keeping myself very busy—cleaning the cooker, hoovering, turning out bedroom cupboards and drawers, brushing cobwebs off ceilings. It was either that or mope around, feeling betrayed. 'Spare me the details,' I said. My voice sounded tinny, like the yapping of a bad-tempered dog.

It is strange how folly attracts disaster, how one bad thing follows another. Perhaps Paul's line of action was the correct one, and we should all have turned our backs on each other and left our children to fend for themselves. Perhaps reconciliation is always faked and there is no such word as 'sorry'. Perhaps if we had all listened more carefully we would have heard the future releasing its safety catch and run for our lives.

'Robin loves you,' Geraldine said while I drifted around like one of the living dead. Robin himself phoned me in the middle of the morning, from the office, to say the same thing. He had navy-blue circles around his eyes, and a bandaged hand and a plaster on the bridge of his nose. 'I walked into a door,' he said when the children asked. 'Some door,' Ray said.

I couldn't bear to see Robin so hopeless and helpless. 'I don't know what possessed me,' he said. 'Was it worth it?' some demon made me ask. I was driven by an unhealthy curiosity to imagine how it had been in the secluded hotel to which they had gone. I remembered the pictures of legs and penises we had seen in a Paris exhibition—erotic octopuses composed of private parts, drawings of transvestites, a case displaying black lingerie and red shoes, a mummy's sarcophagus containing a woman's legs and a huge male member bursting through a froth of black lace. 'Did Geraldine wear her French knickers?' I asked. I remembered their satin extravagance and began to cry. 'Everything is coming unstuck,' I wept. 'No, it's not,' Robin said as he smoothed my hair. I let him convince me.

In my own way I then became as obstinate as Paul. 'We're all adults,' I said to Paul, refusing to be put off by the curl of his lip. He listened to me in silence. I spoke of our families. I said I didn't care if the whole town was laughing, but I wasn't going to wreck my marriage. I told him he was worse than the Ayatollah. I told him that in twenty years time it would all seem funny. I told him that he should never have spied on his wife in the first place, and that he'd reproach himself for the rest of his life if they parted. I said we mustn't be fanatics. I said we'd still be friends always and that Don was like my own son to me. Honest to God! Paul heard me out, rubbing his jaw like a man with a toothache. When I had finished he tilted back his chair and stared up at the office ceiling. 'Robin has been a complete arse-hole,' he said, and I knew I had forced him to relent.

Now I curse myself. Now, thanks to me, Don is dead and Ray is working in a kibbutz.

CHAPTER EIGHT

I had a wicked night. Robin didn't come home until all hours. I was getting ready to organise a search party when he arrived. It didn't help my beauty sleep. I'm exhausted. I feel like a battered old artefact unearthed by an archaeological dig.

'I got up at seven o'clock and I haven't lain down since,' Edna says when I tell her I'm tired.

That's Edna, always one better than you are.

I got up at eight. I lay down on the sofa in the front room in the afternoon. Then I got upset because I was staring up at our Waterford glass chandelier and I remembered the trouble we had assembling it, and how Paul, who was good with his hands, came round one Saturday afternoon and helped Robin to put it up while Geraldine and I iced our Christmas cakes in the kitchen.

Edna insisted on bringing me to this fashion show. I'm carting the eternal mink coat around over my arm because the hotel central heating is on full blast and I don't trust that coat rack in the lobby. I'm wearing a new loosely cut maternity two-piece in black and gold. Nothing to get excited about. It has an Italian label and was so expensive that it was probably made by the same people that make the Pope's vestments.

'It looks beautiful,' Edna says, plucking at my sleeves and skirt as if her sharp eyes are finding pieces of fluff and stray hairs all over the place.

The dead heat makes my head swim. Already my breasts feel as tender and squishy as over-ripe dates.

Robin has gone to a meeting in Kerry with two business colleagues.

Edna catches me by the elbow and points out a woman who, she says, has had her face lifted. If that's true she still has a lot of wrinkles.

'So will we, face lifts or not, by the time we're sixty-one,' Edna says.

She is in a grumpy mood.

By the time I'm sixty-one this lump inside me will be nineteen. Roll on happy day!

'Nineteen,' I said when the policeman asked me what age Ray was. 'They're both nineteen.'

Robin went to Kerry today. If he bumps into Geraldine while he's down there he needn't come back and tell me about it.

I had forgotten how much Edna smokes. When we get to our chairs beside the catwalk she sits on top of me and puffs non-stop.

'I keep trying to give them up but I'm no good at resisting temptation,' she says. After another few drags she adds, 'It's good for us to have a social evening.'

For myself, I'd rather go off somewhere and get tipsy. I'd rather be put in a refugee camp.

All the people here are 'mature ladies' like ourselves. The hall reeks of Femme and Opium. I see May in the distance with Doreen. I'm boiling, but May has her camel coat on over a woollen dress and still looks comfortable. We wave.

It's my luck to be dragged into a photograph for the local paper.

'Mrs who?' 'Oh, Mr King—the insurance man.' Bla . . . bla . . . bla . . .

'Tell him to go to Jericho,' that's the expression Bel used to use when people annoyed her. At least the photograph will be in black and white, the public won't be inflicted with my bright pink face. Go to Jericho, go to Majorca. Edna and Tony are thinking of going to the Canaries. Be philosophical, all this will pass away. The light patches and dark patches all melt into blackness at the end.

I admire Edna's freshly done hairstyle.

She clutches my arm and says, 'Angel, I'm enjoying this. Tony and I don't have good nights-out together. We end up fighting.'

We are still waiting for the fashion show to begin.

Robin and I had an argument this morning because he couldn't find a clean shirt. That's the nearest we come to a fight.

'Honestly, Angel—all men are rotten. You must feel like that— especially now that you're having this baby.'

I turn to look more carefully at Edna. In spite of the freshly washed hair, I can see that she is in bad shape.

As I stare at her, one of her eyes develops a nervous wink, which eventually produces a tear. 'I've discovered that Tony is playing around,' she whispers. There is a pause. 'What would you do?'

Go to Jericho. That's what Bel said, and the walls came tumbling down. 'I'd tell him to go to Jericho.' And why saddle me with this piece of information?

Edna fumbles at her handbag. 'I don't know why I mentioned it. But I'm feeling terrible,' she says.

I can see she's sorry she told me. So am I. There must be several hundred women here who would burst into flames of comfort at this piece of news. Why pick on me?

'She's not even good-looking,' Edna says between sniffs.

'Cheer up,' I say. Edna's squib has made me feel less of a misery myself. Especially when she tells me that the other woman has a job in this very hotel. It is quite comical when I think about it. Other people's misfortunes are easy to bear. 'In another fifty years we'll all be dead,' I say.

'You and I will anyway, and Tony. This one he has is only about your Anne's age. She'll still be going strong,' Edna scrutinises her varnished nails. 'I hope she kills him,' she says bitterly.

I buy some raffle tickets and share them with Edna. 'Perhaps our luck will change,' I say.

'I'm going to send her an anonymous letter.' She folds one of the raffle tickets into a spill as she speaks.

'Be careful! That might be the winning number.'

As it turns out, it is. Edna comes back with a box containing a pair of plated silver goblets. Heads turn in our direction, faces smile.

'Some people have all the luck. What are you going to put in them, Edna?' someone asks.

'Hemlock, in Tony's one,' I say.

There is a shifting of bottoms on stackable chairs, uneasy mothlike glances. I've said the wrong thing. I feel as if I've been stripped of my mink and my new two-piece and that the frayed straps of my old baggy slip are visible to all. I feel as if the make-up on my face has turned into black mud.

I'm relieved when the show recommences, even grateful for the slavish jargon used to describe the fashions. It distracts people, settles things down. And as I'm going to be decidedly pear-shaped myself for some time to come I don't feel called upon to consider seriously the potentiality of the garments offered. I can't see myself in those black shiny satin pyjamas. And neither is that crimson kimono with the tightly tied sash me anymore. I can forget about pink culotte suits, gold lamé sheaths, and navy pencil skirts. I can forget about chic. Slim, slim, slim—that's their message.

I don't know why I'm seeing so much of Edna. I find her as drab as Monday morning, and full of inescapable curiosity.

'How is your friend Noelle? Have you been in Dublin lately?' she whispers as the models parade.

I shrug. 'Noelle? No, I haven't had a chance.'

'How is her little one?'

I don't reply. I'll have to get rid of Noelle, make her flee the country, have her killed.

'Did things turn out alright on her holiday?'

'Shhhh!!' I force back the prying undertow and Edna subsides into a puddle of discontent.

Oh Geraldine, I miss our good times so much I feel tearful as I shift uneasily in my chair, trying to ignore all the flickering worries. I'm not having a baby at all, I'm swollen up with loneliness. I keep expecting you to drop in. It was all Paul's fault, no action should have been taken, nothing said. You were welcome to everything, my hospitality knows no bounds. You can have Leo's testimony as evidence. 'You're an understanding woman, Angel,' he said, 'Robin is very lucky to have such a strong wife.'

I had been describing to him something of the wreckage of the previous months—friends hit by tragedy, our son and their son— my worries about Ray's suppressed guilt, the mad desperation of youthful regrets. 'I'm afraid of what will become of him,' I said. 'We can't persuade him to go back to college.' 'I'll see what I can do,' Leo said. Hester knew people in Israel, she spent five months of every year in Jerusalem. 'Leaving you with a free hand?' I asked.

'Come with me now. I want to take you to bed,' Leo said, then called for the waiter in his best cloak-and-dagger manner. I watched his elegant nervous fingers fiddling with the silver money clip and experienced love as anticipated passion, as a recompense for everything. Leo and I never forced each other's natures. I had used up all my energies in persuading Paul to forgive Geraldine, in letting Robin convince me that for us things could still be the same. With Leo I was on parole from the subsequent trouble, the fright.

The shooting had happened out of the blue. Of course both boys had quick tempers—Don could be as bloody-minded as any of us. But from the first second we had banished any notions of that sort, and there was no point in resurrecting them. 'It just happened, Angel. It was an accident. Never, never, never let yourself think anything else,' Geraldine insisted with stiff-necked energy. Once again she was the strong one, once again she was my closest friend.

Suddenly Edna makes a grab for me and hisses, 'There's Tony's girl.' Edna is not looking at the ramp, she is glaring at the doorway with that horrified stare which people reserve for bad car crashes for instance, when they are forced to see all kinds of things that they don't want to see. 'She plays the piano out in the bar,' Edna mutters.

The plain girl is staring at the show in a dissatisfied manner. If she is so hard to please that a cream tulle wedding dress, heavily flounced, doesn't soften her expression, I don't know what would appeal to her.

'I'm going to speak to her,' Edna says suddenly against the background of music and compère's chat.

I hold onto Edna's sleeve as she struggles to get up from her chair. This is what friends are for. 'Leave it alone,' I say.

'I'm going to tell her to fuck off, she can't come in here without a ticket,' Edna whispers back.

It is a good thing that divorce is not allowed in Ireland. The country is so small that we'd keep bumping into our ex-partners, or the women who had taken our places. Salt in the wound. I'm relieved when Edna sinks back into her chair. I even agree to leave. It is much better to creep out while the show is still in progress even when it does mean a slight disturbance.

It is not until we're crossing the foyer that we remember the silver goblets. We stand in front of the reception desk. Through an archway we can see people lounging in front of a television set.

Police seem to be using awful brutality.

'I'm glad I'm with you, Angel. You're so sensible,' Edna says. She is shaking so hard that her beads and earrings rattle. 'They can keep their silver goblets.'

I'm very tired, as tired as I used to be after the Dublin journey when it became obvious that things between Leo and me were cooling down. What I want is a large cup of coffee, preferably accompanied by a delicious cream cake.

'Do you know what I'm afraid of? I'm afraid that I'll end up by having a nervous breakdown,' Edna says.

The world is full of people who are afraid that they'll end up by having nervous breakdowns. In fact, it is not as easy as they might think. I'd have one myself if I knew how to go about it. I'd shift all the responsibility and turn into a guinea-pig or a white rabbit for the men in the laboratory, instead of blundering along, a self-confessed ass.

We decide that in the circumstances the best thing to do is to go somewhere else for a late drink.

And when we do, Edna harps back to Noelle and her father. I tell her that Noelle's father is very ill.

'What's his surname?'

'Martin.' Invention becomes easier with practice—there is a money box on the pub counter topped by the figure of a black saint. An inscription beneath reads, 'Blessed Martin pray for us.'

Edna always reads the death notices in the paper. She'll look out for Martin. I let her flow on—asking questions while I nibble one of the shrivelled olives that look as if they have lain on a saucer for a long time.

'They're left over from the happy hour,' the barmaid says as she takes our order.

Edna is beginning to forget her own troubles. She wants to know more about Mr Martin's case. Medicine is her thing—her bedroom bookshelf is stacked with medical encyclopaedias, plus books about how to enjoy sex and books about how to keep young.

'Mr Martin is eighty-four ... I don't know whether they operated or not,' I reply to her questions.

I count the olive stones when I have finished. Lady, baby ...

gypsy . . . queen . . . Soon there are empty glasses to match. I've got an uneasy feeling that I'm going to give birth to an agonised old man instead of a squalling brat. Right now Mr Martin and the child in my womb are concepts of equal value. Well, as far as paternity is concerned they are both figments of the imagination. As far as Edna and Mr Martin, and Robin and 'his' child are concerned anyway. It's a wise child that knows its own father. Not that it matters. It is the basic ingredient that counts. I'm feeling philosophical after all these drinks. 'Here's to life,' I say, lifting my whiskey glass. It occurs to me that I didn't have very much to eat all day. A slice of ham, a few cubes of cheese, an apple—and these olives which seem to have lodged in my chest.

Edna isn't at all interested in my optimistic approach. She stops speaking, stares at me curiously, and then—as tears well up again—says, 'You're priceless, Angel.'

Thanks, but I'm not. And Edna is getting me down. I wish it was Geraldine with her coppery hair who was sitting here beside me, both of us having a good laugh.

We should have gone into the hotel piano-bar after all, cocked a snook at the pianist. This isn't our kind of place. Everything seems dusty. I'm beginning to feel slightly olive green.

Edna launches into a discussion of the dresses in the show—I should have paid more attention. What was that about favourite in the harem? Talking to Edna—or May, or any of the coffee ladies—is like going for a paddle instead of having a good swim. 'You're priceless, Angel,' accompanied by a smirky grin. And they all have those buttoned up titters. Although I must say Edna took me by surprise out in the hotel with her 'fuck off'. That was overheard. That will be held against her. I saw her getting the sort of glances you get when you speak too loudly in the library. Not that Edna goes to the library, all she reads are those medical encyclopaedias and the sex and beauty manuals.

The place has started to empty. The barmaid returns to collect the dirty glasses and the saucer of olive stones.

'They were lovely,' I say, although they have made me full of wind.

Edna is speaking in derogatory terms about her piano-playing rival. It is time we went home. I wish I could catch the barmaid's eye and ask her the way to the bathroom. Or perhaps I should go straight to the hospital . . . I'd give anything to put my head down on a pillow. I'm the very opposite of the princess and the pea in the fairy-story, I'd even sleep like a top on a mattress stuffed with olive stones . . .

I don't know what brought us into this place. If you look at it aesthetically, it is a perfect example of lack of taste . . .

'Can I get you ladies a taxi?' The owner of the bar must think that we're celebrities. He comes over and asks us this without even introducing himself.

We're both quite happy lolling here on his banquette. And I'm feeling much better. That last drink did the trick. The olives are now floating around as comfortably as my baby. 'Jewish girls are the most beautiful girls in the world.' I felt a quiver of pain when Leo said that. Not so much for myself, but because it seemed so unfair to Anne and Jenny . . .

'You're forcing me to call the guards,' the owner says.

He should be glad of our custom . . .

The latter part of the evening has flown. Robin will probably be at home when I get there.

'Come on, fatty,' the owner says.

He's a young man with no respect for ladies. That's why he tosses my mink coat at me so roughly. I'm aware that Edna is leaving by the side exit. The front door seems to be locked. There's no one in the place except myself and this barrack-square monster. I'm afraid he's a bit cuckoo. I find it difficult to get into my coat.

'Sorry, missus, you're pickled,' he says. 'You should be at home saying the rosary.'

I don't know why we came into his filthy little bar. As soon as I have my mink safely on I tell him what I think of it. I don't care whether he agrees with me or not.

I say nothing as I climb into the car beside Edna. We don't speak until we get back to my house.

'Next time round we'll go somewhere more pleasant,' Edna says as I get out of the car.

Jenny is in the kitchen filling a hot-water bottle. 'Anne phoned,' she says.

I've got the hiccups.

Robin is upstairs, asleep with the radio playing.

This must be how an astronaut feels in space. I've walked across the room and it is as if I've run a grinding marathon. My legs feel funny. My fingers that clutch the back of the bedroom chair are as stiff and dry as a bunch of rattan.

I've been here for three or four days, all thanks to those mysterious olives. It must have been the olives. Edna says she had no after-effects. The past few days are a blurred canvas. Nothing definite has happened except that I seem more of a tub than ever.

We're only half-way through March. We haven't even reached St Patrick's Day when I've recovered enough to come downstairs. I'm left with Jenny for company while Robin goes to a Lions' Club meeting. 'Company' is hardly accurate. Jenny is acting withdrawn and strange. The best thing to do is ignore her, keep your distance unless you're wearing kid gloves. She is as prickly as a cactus plant. The resemblance is emphasised by her latest spiky haircut.

'Where's the new jacket I bought you for Christmas?' I ask.

She is wearing a grimy green thing with badges stuck on its sleeves and all the buttons missing from the pocket flaps. Olive green—looking at it makes me feel queasy.

'It's too small.'

I don't believe her. 'Where on earth did you get that grubby thing?'

'I bought it.'

It seems you can buy other people's used clothes in a back lane. It is the most hopeless garment imaginable.

'How much?'

Jenny refuses to answer.

She is worse than unsociable, she is downright snotty. An adolescent at crisis point, that's all an expectant mother of my age needs to make life perfect. 'Why don't you buy yourself something nice?' I can remember a cherry-red coat with a white fur collar.

'I've no money.'

'I'll give you money for whatever you need.'

'I don't need anything.'

You need a good smack on your backside, miss.

CHAPTER NINE

I take the red car out as far as the cottage.

Anne is playing hostess to Bridget and a girl with blonde curls whom they introduce as Maxie. I feel awkward, coming in on the three young women, uninvited. Bridget is wearing a brown felt hat with a neat brim, the sort of hat I shrank from as a schoolgirl. On her it is attractive and flighty. The three of them are in a giddy mood—they chatter and wave their arms about. There is a wine bottle on the sideboard and another one, empty, on the goatskin rug.

'Brian will kill me,' Anne says, adding that he is going to New York on business so she has taken the day off to get his things ready.

'Then we called, and so we're having a wine-and-cheese party instead—except that there is no cheese,' Bridget says.

'I used it for the scallops mornay,' Anne says and then giggles.

'Why should he kill you? You make him sound like the Arabs,' Maxie protests. 'I was nearly killed by an Arab. He pulled a dagger on me.' She yawns and jangles an armful of beaded bracelets. She is a very pretty girl with a made-up face that is cleverly rouged and glimmers in the right places.

'Maxie spent three months tramping in the Middle East,' Anne says.

I take a mouthful of wine—it is harsh bitter stuff. 'I think I'll just have a glass of water,' I say to Anne.

When I go out into the kitchen there is a pause, and then Bridget says something in a low voice. I hear their glasses clinking. I stand at the sink, a lorry lumbers past the gate. The girls are chattering like magpies. There are scallop shells in the sink basket and some dinner plates and a bowl containing some pink spongy mixture on the draining board. A cookery book lies open on the Welsh dresser at the meat dishes section, and there are grocery bags and two courgettes on the kitchen table.

I have no business here, I haven't even bought food for ourselves. I call, 'Goodbye,' with my hand on the doorknob.

'See you.'

'See you soon!'

'Bye-e-e-e!'

Outside, dried up hydrangeas rattle in the flower-bed as Brian, wearing a smart waterproof hat, hurries in the gate. I mutter a greeting as we pass each other by.

In town, in the butcher's shop on the corner, a young pregnant African woman, with caste marks scored on her cheeks, buys an oxtail, and haggles about the price with a terrified assistant. When she stalks out we gape at each other, temporarily dazzled.

In the basement supermarket a boy pushes a checkout girl out of the way, scoops up a handful of money from her cash register and dashes up the stairs. All the other girls leave their checkouts to go and see the excitement.

I get home and I find I have left the bag with the steaks from the butcher's shop in the supermarket. Cherry log, fillet steak—what the hell! 'Don't handle food that you are not going to buy,' warned the printed notice in the cake shop. The apple tart that I bring home looks as if it has been sat on.

There is still a long while until teatime. My back aches as if I had slept on rocks. I press the television button and get the test card. When the station does comes on the air most of the programmes one way or the other seem to consist of people talking about abortion.

'I want to assure every woman who may be watching that in Holles Street Hospital she will receive appropriate treatment for her condition, whether or not she is pregnant at the time.'

'If a doubtfully-live grenade is found on the pathway, it would be grossly immoral to throw it into the porch of a doubtfully-occupied house.'

And similar nonsense.

'I'm having Leo's baby!' I say at the top of my voice to the four walls and the box in the corner.

Nothing happens. No priest or politician crawls out of the screen. Everything continues to lie in place. I grant you that the weather seems to have changed its mind—I can see a patch of blue. Perhaps the blue patch is a sign, a token. It is big enough for a pair of sailor's trousers. But I want something more spectacular—a Star of David, or my car turned into a fiery chariot—before I'll acknowledge this child's father. Sorry lads, but that's the way it goes. As far as you're concerned there is nothing concrete unless I say so.

Nothing has come of that blue bit, instead here comes a torrential shower. I'm glad that I have a roof over my head.

I stand by the curtains, looking out. The rain is so heavy that it hisses. Everyone on the road must be indoors, cleaning house, making tea. I'd make tea if I had Nancy here to read the tea-leaves. She inherited the gift from her mother. I'd get her to tell me if all will go well. On second thoughts, I wouldn't. She might see more thàn I wanted her to.

Nancy wore a most unNancyish red dress, bright and sexy, the night that she read Ray's cup. That occasion is as clear in my mind as a photograph. I can even remember the date. And the dead silence after Ray and Don, unimpressed, went off to look for some better entertainment. Nancy in a red dress sailing like a blood red moon across the kitchen. Her grim face and the way she rinsed the cup out immediately. And the next evening, after I had put her on the Dublin train . . . Why couldn't she have told me what she had seen before it happened? I'd have locked Ray up in his room, forever if necessary.

It is better to drown your sorrows, in the hope that if they are completely submerged for long enough barnacles will make them look like something else. I tried my best—attended approximately forty cocktail parties, refused to admit that faces didn't light up when I approached. Well, my perseverance has paid off—this baby has thrown everything else into the shade.

'Things should go like clockwork,' Billy Black said last time I saw him. I believe him. Both Ray and Jenny arrived into the world at the same time as Billy turned up in the nursing home, coolly finishing off a tub of ice-cream, I'm told, as he sauntered into the labour ward. Anyhow, the nurses do everything. He just supervises.

Oh, I'm looking forward to the celebration. I'll have a party with a tiny dark yum-yum baby as centrepiece. We have always enjoyed fêtes, have even made something special out of Hallowe'en when Geraldine and Paul were here. Hey—I'm not going to be a fat mama for ever, this gigantic tummy is just the hors-d'oeuvre. As long as the four of us were together it didn't matter much who else came along. May and Albert, Edna and Tony, a friendly plumber who was passing through. We had some wonderful times, especially when Paul sang. 'Strangers in the night'. 'I did it my way'. 'Alone, all alone—tum tum'. 'She moved through the fair'. 'I met my thrill on Blueberry Hill,' until we discovered that the bar had closed.

And then something completely unexpected happened. Something that could have been avoided by a fractional shift in either direction. You spend another second in bed and when you get up you're pregnant. You telephone instead of calling round or *vice versa*, in which case your car collides with a bicycle. Afterwards you could be knocked down by a feather.

'Your father is dead.' That was the message that Robin gave me after he had answered the Roman waiter's hammering. I didn't cry. In fact I lay down as if I was half-asleep. The room seemed full of heavy-footed people. It was probably because of the thumping in my head. The awful thing was that I didn't want to go home at all. I wouldn't have cared if I had never got the message. I wanted to visit the Tivoli Gardens by night, take a horse-drawn carriage up the Via Veneto. There were the markets, and coffee beans in the sambuca glass. Without me Robin would be seduced by a pretty girl riding a Lambretta. I had to throw my three coins into the fountain.

If I had been the one to answer the door I would have returned to bed and said nothing. I knew how to keep a secret. I'd have said, 'That's awful. No. We never got the message at all.' The only person I cared about in the situation—my father—was beyond being hurt by any off-handedness on my part. He wouldn't have wanted my honeymoon spoilt at any cost. As it was, in no time, Robin had rustled up some extra lire and bought me an air ticket so that I'd make it home in time for the funeral.

Off I went on the early bus to the airport while Robin remained in the piazza watching the water from the fountain splash the Lambretta girls. At first I was inclined to think that the waiter's nocturnal intrusion was some bawdy honeymoon joke. (After one-and-a-half days in Italy I had had my bottom squeezed several times.) I never even suspected that anything was amiss until Robin said to me, 'Your father is dead.'

I sat in the airport that morning feeling like something that had been mislaid. A young soldier bought me an orange juice. 'I am a married woman,' I said. He said a word I didn't understand, and walked away.

Sure, my father had taken to using a walking stick and his stomach made rumbling noises after a few mouthfuls of dinner. He had been in hospital in Dublin for a few days, but there had been no operation. Of course he had grown thin, but the thought of a serious illness had never crossed my mind.

'The funeral is at half-past two,' Mr King said. He took off his hat when he spoke to me. He was very pleased because it was Miss Hurley herself who telephoned Rome from the drapery shop. 'Young Miss Hurley, personally,' he said. He and Mrs King and Nancy all walked up to the station to meet the train. It was the first time in my life I had found myself a fully-established member of a family group.

This all comes back to me as I answer the telephone which has been ringing for ages. It's a good thing, after all, that I didn't stay with Anne for too long. The hospital phoned earlier and got no reply. The reason that they tried again is because there doesn't seem to be anyone else to whom it might matter. Bel died in her sleep early this morning.

Well, that's just marvellous. 'No. I'm fine really.' I'm shattered, of course.

'She had a hard time, but the end was quick,' the voice says. It sounds like the description of a pregnancy.

Then I put down the telephone and start to feel awful. I find it difficult to put my thoughts into any sort of order. I grab some things—toothpaste, cold-cream, a nightie, a black chiffon scarf with a gold thread—and put them in a suitcase. I can't think of anything for tea except bread and cheese and the squashed apple tart.

The clock in the dining-room strikes six and I hear Robin's key in the door. Thank goodness he is home at a civilised hour. I'll never forget that early-morning trip out to Rome airport, and how horrible the smell of garlic is first thing in the morning.

Robin thinks of all the things that I have forgotten, such as ringing Nancy. And Jenny and Anne will come along as well. Anything to swell the crowd, and give Bel some kind of a send-off.

CHAPTER TEN

Nancy is waiting for us in the foyer of the hotel. She is going to
have a field-day. She taps a cigarette against her pigskin cigarette
case and says, 'Well, this is a kettle of fish.'

'Hello, Aunt Nancy,' Anne says.

Jenny goes over and kisses her. I notice how the expensive jade-
green woollen dress accentuates Nancy's pigeon-chest.

She catches my hand and presses it so hard that her many rings
dig into my skin. 'My dear,' she says.

We exchange an unenthusiastic embrace. At least the business
of telling her that I'm pregnant is over, I told her on the telephone
at the same time as I told her that Bel was dead. Trust Nancy, whose
brown eyes are her one agreeable feature, to get blue-rimmed
butterfly spectacles, and to put on puce lipstick against her strong
but yellowish teeth. It isn't her mother that Nancy reminds me of,
standing in the hotel lobby, feet apart, leaning back from the hips,
making pronouncements.

'I'm still trying to get over the shock of all your news . . . I'd have
known something was wrong, Angel, even if you hadn't told me,
you poor wretch . . . For a person in your position, Robin, I must
say you have acted carelessly.'

Anne and Jenny have disappeared up to their bedrooms.

'We haven't time for talk right now, Nancy,' I say, 'we have to
get over to the nursing home.'

We stop the car bonnet-to-bonnet with a hearse complete with
empty coffin. I think it is for Bel, but she has already been put in
hers. This place has a lot of commerce with undertakers. No
wonder the two fellows unloading the new one look so tired, it's
from carting dead bodies away, day in, day out.

There is a packed suitcase and a few things—towel, soap—on

Bel's vacated bed.

'I think that's everything,' the nurse says.

I open the suitcase—old clothes, a Post Office book, some screws of newspaper, a copy of *Kim* by Rudyard Kipling, and a large silver serving spoon with my mother's family initials on the handle. I take the spoon and the Post Office book. Everything else can be thrown away. Robin has checked the arrangements. Bel is going to be buried in the same graveyard as our parents. No one knows where the husband in Camden was laid to rest. I feel made of ice as the black-browed nurse leads me down to the mortuary where Bel lies. Robin comes with me. Nancy and the girls remain in the front parlour. We look at the shrivelled whiteness, the wispy wings of hair, the furled, concealing gown.

I never liked this nurse. She is the sort of person I wouldn't mind hearing bad news about. That she had been attacked in an alleyway by a drunk, for instance. Not a dangerous drunk, not a rapist, just a drunk. She seems to take pleasure from the way Bel's corpse leaves us strained and exhausted.

'Oh, please!' I say to Robin. I am terrified that a sound ('Angel. H-e-e-l-p!') will come from between Bel's lips, which are just the tiniest unfortunate bit open.

'All we can do for her now is pray,' the nurse says insidiously.

Exactly. I can see she is criticising me—us—the general set-up. I can feel her pushing me to admit some undefined irregularity. For all I know, she could be a girl from hereabouts and well aware of the circumstances. Those heavy-browed women are common in the locality, I know the type. The sins of the fathers, *ad infinitum*. I'm not going to create a to-do for her edification.

I reach out and put my hand on Bel's arm and feel the icy chill through the grave clothes. My father's woman. I admit it silently. Why didn't I bring her down to Limerick for a holiday—give her a break? She'd have liked to come down, especially when she had the use of her legs, but I didn't encourage it.

Sometimes, something quite unexpected shocks you into complete composure. That's the effect touching Bel in her coffin has on me. I am able to match beastliness with beastliness. It is the nurse who walks behind us on the way back to the parlour to collect Nancy and the girls. It is her shoes that skid nervously on the linoleum as we cross the hall.

There has obviously been some sort of row in our absence because Anne is saying, 'Oh shit!' as we open the door.

I pretend not to hear and concentrate on Nancy, who looks in a villainous mood. I admire her hat, a trilby affair with some spiky black feathers stuck into its brim. I have nothing for my head so Nancy insists that I tie on the chiffon scarf that she pulls from her handbag.

'It looks all wrong,' Jenny says. She is wearing the belt of her dress as a headband.

'At least I don't look like an Indian brave,' I say.

Anne squeezes her hands together and stares at the empty fireplace. She is wearing pink slacks and a short leather jacket.

'Even so, Jenny has enough respect for the dead to wear a dress instead of trousers,' Nancy says.

'Bel wouldn't have minded,' I answer.

Nancy cackles and says, 'Oh, Bel . . .' then pulls her face into sanctimonious folds as she sees Bel's coffin being carried across the hall.

There are a handful of people waiting in the local church. Most of them look unfamiliar, but I do remember Eugene Prendergast. He was the bright boy in the tennis club when I was growing up. I was always promising him that I'd go to the pictures with him instead of with Robin. Now he is the parish clerk. I feel as if we're at a fancy-dress party, Robin, Eugene and I, all togged out in grown-ups' clothes. Although Jenny deserves the prize for her pointy-toed bootees and the black woolly stockings under the flouncy braided skirt, not to mention the headband. At least she has left the revolting green combat jacket at home.

There was a summer while I was growing up during which I seemed to meet Eugene wherever I went. And a fracas in the tennis club because he crossed Robin's name off a list for a tournament. Eugene Prendergast—plump, nervous, going to seed, but more memorable than the other ancient ghosts who flit out of the church shadows to press their sympathy.

'It's too bad, Angel.' Eugene holds my hand in the old way for so long that I have to pull away because of his soft sweaty palm.

If you count ourselves, there are about twelve people present. There is Mrs Delmage, who should be dead years ago, I recognise her big hat and pebble glasses immediately. She must have kept track of every funeral and wedding in the district since the year dot. 'I'll never forget those theatrical gentlemen at your mother's funeral, dearie,' she used to croon. 'Strange gentlemen, beautiful gentlemen. Oh, she was a silly girl, your mother.'

Nancy throws an eye over the gathering. 'Not a bad crowd, considering.'

'Considering what?' I say sharply.

I see a young boy with a fat bottom and a chubby serious face in the group. He is so like Eugene that he has to be his son. You couldn't miss the resemblance, even down to the cleft in his chin. Funny when a child is a replica of its father. That's the sort of thing old curiosity boxes like Mrs Delmage poke out. 'Where did you get him from? Don't try to fool me. Look at the nose. Look at the colouring. The Kings never had those fingers.' I can imagine the old bag, relentless as a bad fairy.

I must keep bright and breezy, and calm and subdued, as befits the occasion.

Where was Moses when the lights went out, riddle me that, Mrs Delmage. 'Is that the brassy one who lives with your father?' a bygone query of Mrs Delmage's rings in my ears.

'Oh, my brothers and sisters—mm . . . mmm . . .' We mumble our prayers in the afternoon gloom.

'Pray for me, Mrs Delmage.'

'Pray for me, Angel.'

Brassy Bel is listening. Honest to God, you should all be on the stage with your 'mm . . . mmm . . .' Pretending to lift me sky-high, then back to your mixed grills and cakes, your whiskeys and gin. I haven't been interested in prayers since Don died, I've stopped believing that they can change things. Mmm . . . mmm . . . We all need our heads examined. All I can see are words guttering away like spent wicks—and then the dark. I'd laugh if the coffin lid opened and Bel sat up.

My mind is divided about what I'll have when we get to the hotel. Gin or sherry?

The matron in the hospital said that she believed there were some larger effects in storage someplace. I have our silver spoon. I try to think what else could have been left in Bel's possession after the auction? The stuff that arrived on a cart after she had lived with my father for a couple of months? A few bits of ornamental delft, a wardrobe with a badly blistered inlay of bows and festoons and a mirror that turned you a funny shape, a gnome-sized dressing-table, an elegant occasional table.

Geraldine knew all about Bel. Over the years we had given each other full details of our respective histories. We used to sit in each other's houses, unwinding until we were little girls again. She gave me her Auntie Olive and a younger aunt—a simpleton who spent her time crocheting clothes for Geraldine's dolls—so I handed over Bel. We swopped schooldays—Geraldine had been afraid that she would go to hell because of her hatred of Sister Benedict, and the very title 'Mother Ignatius' still makes my innards lurch. Her favourite uncle owned a pub, so I told her about the Kings because I didn't know my own relations. (My mother's family did not speak to us, and my father—who had spent many years in India as a young man—just never bothered to contact his people when he returned.)

Geraldine had two brothers called Sean and Barney, and a sister called Peg. She didn't have anything in common with the boys and Peg had gone to Canada. I told of how I had always got on better with Robin than with Nancy. She said, 'And I worked in the same firm as Paul for several years before I could stand the sight of him. I didn't know until after we had slept with each other that he was right for me.' She offered this revelation as carelessly as she had tried on her French knickers for my benefit, dispatching the whole business of premarital sex with a snap of her fingers. Robin and I had never dared to try anything until after we married. This Geraldine refused to understand. 'How on earth could you take such a gamble?' she asked. There were certain moments when, even with Geraldine, I could find no explanation. Perhaps it had something to do with Bel, perhaps I believed too sincerely in the marriage system. I certainly never saw Geraldine as a rival any more than I allowed Bel to take my mother's place.

So what happened? When I have a bad shock my period usually starts, right when I don't want it. After Don's death I started bleeding heavily and irregularly. That is one of the snags of the Billings method—all summer Robin couldn't come near me. And yet at the same time, with Leo, I acted as if I was a perfectly normal twentieth-century woman, who was interested in a little light dalliance. 'Sex is always good between friends,' Leo said as I lay with my mind and my legs wide open. I agreed. I wanted to benefit from its passionate extravagance. I wanted to grasp the world by the scruff of the neck and shake its pockets empty. The previous months had cost me dear, now it was my turn to collect. And look what I got!

I can't stand the church any longer. I clutch Robin's arm and moan, 'Get me out of this.'

'We can't just rush off,' Robin whispers back.

We haven't eaten since early morning, but Robin is right. Having come so far we can't just whisk away from the church. I study the flowers—Nancy's sheaf, our big wreath, one of those transparent crosses full of wax blossoms, and the matron's bunch of narcissi. It is a fair enough display. Add to this my mink and we must look respectable enough to satisfy Mrs Delmage.

Eugene Prendergast is staring at me. I must look a fright—part-knowing, part-afraid. Like up in his parents' bedroom that time when the house was empty. He took the big bolster from under the pillows and placed it in the middle of the bed. Its overstuffed look reminded me immediately of his mother. He promised he'd leave it there if I took off my clothes and lay down. He'd keep the bolster between us the whole time if I'd just let him look, cross his heart and hope to die. I didn't stay. I went up to our house and leafed through *Treasure Island* which Robin had lent me. I found it boring, but it was an improvement on Eugene. I decided to go and look for Robin in the vacuum of the summer afternoon.

We are back in the hotel.

'Angel is a bit shocked,' Robin is saying to Nancy.

I'm not shocked. I just don't want any post-mortems. And Jenny
is looking at her bacon and scrambled egg with the same appalled
expression she had when they lowered Bel's coffin into the hole in
the ground. 'God help her!' a voice whispered as Jenny screamed.
Now I find that, like Jenny, I can't eat.

I say, 'It's better for Bel than being in that place. It wasn't what
you'd call a holiday home.'

Jenny catches her breath.

I say, 'I wonder who sent that awful waxy cross?'

Jenny cries, 'Oh, that's typical!'

Anne says, 'I forgot to bring any.' Her eyes are red.

My scrambled egg has congealed into a wet pus. I wish they'd
come and collect our plates. The standards of this place aren't up
to scratch. I notice the shoddiness, the flaking green distemper, the
dirty washcloth used to swipe away crumbs. You should see our
bedroms—artificial stones set into a powder-blue wall, grimy
hessian, and built-in Regency. We will be off first-thing in the morning.

'I suppose that Miss Anne here can't wait to get back to her
amour,' Nancy says. Nancy drank two large scotches with her tea.
They have whetted her temper. 'I must be on the road,' she adds.

I imagine her driving home across the Curragh, thinking of all
the other fine things she could have said. I get to my feet. 'I'm going
to see Nancy to her car.' I force the words out, my mouth feels as
tight as a rusty pin. I pick up Nancy's handbag from the table and
start to walk away.

She follows me—like a dog following someone with a bone. 'It's
a great shame that Ray couldn't be here, Bel always did like boys
much better than girls,' Nancy says as we stand by her car with
the breeze whipping our cheeks and our noses dripping from the
cold. 'I'm very disappointed about this expected baby on top of
everything else,' she says. 'I thought that you and Robin had more
sense.'

I figure that if I say nothing at all she has no choice but to get
into her car and drive away.

'I'm sorry that I didn't know. Tony and I would have gone up for the funeral,' Edna says sincerely.

Even so, I'm sure she doesn't mean it. She has called in with a mass card, but she didn't know what name to put on it so instead of getting one for the dead she got one for my intentions.

'We go to more funerals than parties nowadays,' she says stoically.

I don't like to ask how things are between herself and Tony.

'I can't abide funerals, except Protestant ones. They have lovely hymns. Ours are too gloomy—all those condolences, everyone wanting to know the gruesome details,' she says.

Then May turns up. It is eleven o'clock in the morning and Robin expects to be fed at lunchtime.

'I always cry no matter who it is,' Edna says. She is arguing with May, who says a funeral should be a celebration.

'You should do what I do,' May says, referring to Robin's lunch.

May makes a big supply of sandwiches every Sunday night and puts them in her freezer. That's it as far as fixing lunch is concerned in her house. In Edna's case, Tony has his lunch in the airport canteen—or maybe, these days, with his ladyfriend.

'Did Noelle come down from Dublin for the funeral?' May asks.

There is something greasy about May's grin this morning, something I don't care for.

I move to dig some potatoes out of the paper sack and then instead I sit down on a stool and begin to cry. I cry the way I should have cried all through the funeral mass, and down the aisle after the coffin. This is what you could call delayed shock. This is the irrational behaviour of a woman having a baby instead of the menopause.

Edna holds on to me until I become sensible, while May pours gins and tonics for the three of us. I'm regretful because, in the graveyard, I wasn't brave enough to go over and look at my parents' tombstone. It was put up by my mother's family. It gives her age—twenty-six, and her name—Sophie Stone, *née* Rivers. As far as I know, my father's name has never been added. I didn't know how to go about it—but he is there, where he belongs, beside her whether they like it or not.

But now with some gin and tonic inside me I don't feel so bad.

I don't even mind those snowflakes melting on the windowpane
and the washing stiff on the line. When I think of Bel tucked in
against the cemetery wall and Father and Mother up near the
Calvary figures it just seems bizarre.

The hall-door shuts behind May and Edna. The gin bottle is
empty—so much for close friends. The telephone rings—it is
Anne—and the hall-door opens again—it is Jenny—at the same
time.

'I'm fine. I'm feeling grand.' I smile at Jenny as I speak into the
mouthpiece.

She tramps past me, scowling, on her way to the bathroom.

Next I pick up the empty tampon cylinders left lying on the
bathroom floor as usual. At least it shows that Jenny's problem isn't
a teenage pregnancy.

CHAPTER ELEVEN

And now the flu epidemic has struck. Everyone has it, including myself. We lie in bed, somnolent and miserable, while dirty soup bowls clutter our bedside tables and lemon slices studded with cloves dry up in cloudy drinking glasses. All I want is peace.

I have a persistent hum in my ear. It is eventually diagnosed as the electric clock behind my cold-cream jar. I smear vaseline on chapped lips.

A wintery sun gilds the sky and Nancy's car pulls up at the gate. She arrives at my bedside carrying a paper bag. It contains a cherry log. I can't even look at it. Nancy has some time off. She thinks that, with me out of action, it is her duty to come down. And Robin and Jenny are sick as well.

'You'd think Anne would come in and give a hand,' Nancy says.

'Anne has her own life to live,' I defend her.

Nancy is a nuisance. She doesn't know where the shops are, she doesn't know which chemist to go to.

'Every other house on the road has its bedroom blinds pulled,' Nancy says.

I'm thinking of Bel, of how lucky she is to be dead. I don't care if I die tomorrow. I won't be able for the horrors of encroaching age if I'm spared indefinitely. I want Robin near me and at least one or two friends and the children.

'When you're better we'll go on a Greek cruise,' Robin promises.

'Complete with baby?'

Robin is better so he has to go into the office.

I don't know if it is midnight or midday. Outside it seems to be raining non-stop. I wake up from a snooze to find the tomcat beside me in the bed. He puts my heart crossways. I'm glad I don't believe in reincarnation, he could so easily be someone you know. Wow!

I reach out and shove him off the pillow. He stalks away, waving his plumy tail, leaving me on my litter. He has my number. Why didn't I go over to England and have a simple operation, that's what he'd like to know. Do I realise that I haven't the monopoly on motherhood?

I hear sounds of shifting metal. A man's voice jabbers at the window.

'The window cleaner,' Nancy says. She hired him.

St Patrick's Day is over and spring is on the way. There are all kinds of odds and ends to be attended to, but I lie here, the fat lady in the amusement arcade ignoring the peepers. 'It is a very bad flu and being pregnant doesn't help,' Billy Black said.

'I'd arranged to go back to Dublin tomorrow, but a few more nights won't matter,' Nancy says.

My nose is in a pulp from paper tissues.

' . . . Dee Vee,' Nancy says on the telephone. 'She'll be herself in another few days, Dee Vee.'

Perhaps I should make my will.

'She gave us the fright of our lives,' Nancy says into the mouthpiece.

A piano keeps jangling in my head although, since Ray left, nobody plays our piano. It waits silently between the fireplace and window. I try not to notice it too much, except when I'm dusting.

'I'm not used to all this pot-walloping, I haven't had as much practice as Angel,' Nancy complains to Robin.

She has had a row with Betty, and now we have no cleaning woman. The absence of Betty, and her routine—Monday for washing, Tuesday for downstairs, and so on about the house—adds to the air of unreality. Robin drove out to her cottage to plead with her but got no further than her brother. Betty doesn't want to know us anymore. I don't blame her. I suppose she couldn't stand being quizzed through those blue-butterfly spectacle frames any more than I can.

'Nancy always looks as if there's a bad smell,' I say. 'If I die having this child you can get her to come down and mind you and Jenny full-time.'

I probably will die. How wise I was not to tell Robin about my infidelity. One sperm is the same as another, why discriminate? We all belong to the same zoo. 'There's not a fear of you, Angel,' Billy Black said. The only thing wrong is that my fingers seem to have become thin from inactivity. So thin that my wedding ring is loose. 'Now people will take you for an unmarried mother,' Robin said, while the ring made a small gold protest on top of my jewel-box.

I begin to wheeze like a bellows. 'No, I'm alright.' It is just something that is always a hair's breadth away. 'I used to be terrified in case Bel landed a stepbrother or sister on me,' I say.

I'd have smothered it in its pram. I'd have gone crazy. Nancy once told me that her mother said that my mother had been completely bats. I never had the courage to ask anyone else if it was true. My father said she died of a kidney infection. People don't die of kidney infections nowadays, but they crack up faster than ever.

'Maybe they weren't able to have a child,' Robin says.

Maybe Bel had more sense than I had about the safe period. Maybe, even in those days, there were such things as diaphragms. 'Bats', the word hangs like a lump of mourning crêpe over my mother as I deliberately cut myself off.

Life suddenly seems full of time. I wander over my private battlefield, leisurely munching a chicken sandwich, feeling the emptiness of the house now that Nancy has gone. Neither a skull nor severed limb in sight—except when I switch on the television and see them all blasting each other to bits in the Middle East. Even so, I'm optimistic that Ray will come home in one piece. Nancy has sworn that he will. I capitulated, and wheedled her into reading my teacup. 'Someone close to you will shortly give you a happy surprise. It's a young man. He is dark. There is a woman beside him.' The 'young' excludes Leo and Robin, I don't know any dark young men except Ray, I'm not interested in the woman. My mind is settled.

'I feel Ray will be home before the summer,' I say, throwing a straw to Robin as I kiss him goodbye.

He is off to County Kerry again.

I can't even manage to sound sympathetic when Edna rings with the news that May's husband is still seriously ill after having had flu.

'Poor old Albert, I suppose he needs love too,' I quip, sorry if I sound flippant.

As for Jenny, it's fifty-fifty.

'How much weirder can you get?' I ask when she descends wearing safety-pin jewellery.

'Try looking at yourself,' she answers, and runs.

Of course I'll have to get someone new to help me clean the house. Just one room and I'm dead. You could write your name in the dust. I prove it by tracing out 'Leo' on the sideboard. It seems like something done by a *doppelgänger*. I have to move everything, Mr King's silver teapot and all, to dust it properly.

'Hi!' Anne appears at the other side of the table. 'What are you doing?'

'This room is a disgrace,' I say, polishing furiously as my face reddens.

Anne wrinkles her forehead and I keep polishing until the top of the sideboard begins to look like brown glass. She stares as if fascinated while I put back the silver.

'What's all this polishing about?' she asks.

'I'm getting obsessive. I don't know if it's middle-age or pregnancy,' I say to excuse myself. I am concerned to see how drawn she looks, I hope she isn't catching a bug. 'How are things in the cottage?' I ask. 'How are your friends—Bridget, Maxie?' I'm pleased with myself for remembering their names.

Anne turns away from me and whistles between her teeth.

'Your grandad always said that a whistling woman and a crowing hen—'

'I know. I know.' She stops whistling and begins to play a mock tune on the tabletop. 'You should be sitting down instead of dusting,' she says abruptly.

I know, my dear. I know. But when I sit down such strange

fantasies and imaginings begin. And it is not just me, everyone has them. The last time your father and I went to the films we saw a movie in which a woman suckled a strange man in a railway carriage and later stuck a gun up her vagina and blew herself to pieces.

'I just dropped in for a second, I'm cooking a meal for some of Brian's friends so I have to go to the shopping centre. I thought I might be able to pick up some things for you as well.'

I can't think of anything that I need.

When she has gone I try making a sample list. Powder, cream, napkins (I know nothing about these paper jobs which they advertise by singing commercial jingles while we are eating our breakfast), gowns, shawls, bottles, teats, gripe water, whiskey—anything to keep it quiet at night. Losing my sleep does terrible things to me. I remember the thalidomide scandal. Poor little creatures with flippers instead of arms and legs—all grown-ups by now. It was rumoured that the drug had been perfected in Nazi concentration camps by experimenting on baby Jews. And so on, and so on, glycerine to cool hot little gums.

The list seems so incredibly boring that I cross it all out and scribble down Leo's telephone number. So much water has flown under the bridge that I don't think I would recognise his voice. I need this baby as much as I need a broken leg. What I need is a holiday. If Robin had taken me to Rome in September instead of October this might never have happened. He is so safe that he decided that we should wait until October. It was too late by the time we landed in that huge double bed. Even the damp patch on the wall outside the shower seemed to take on the shape of Leo's profile as I lay awake after lunch while Robin snored. All the frills—siesta, sambuca and coffee beans, were coals to Newcastle. I begged off lovemaking. 'My period seems to be late. I'm sorry it has to be like this,' I bluffed.

I tear the list and Leo's telephone number into confetti. I must think of all my blessings! Take the children's allowance in this wonderful country of ours, another eleven or twelve pounds per month added onto the family budget of hundreds. How about that for largesse! Eleven Irish punts and twenty-five Irish pees, missus—and don't spend it all in the one shop. It is an insult to the ladies of the parish. I believe that single mothers get more, but let's face it, not much more—not enough to put a roof over my head. Bless me, father, for I have sinned—infidelity. Avoid the occasion of sin, my child, and for your penance, eleven-point-two-five punts plus the five joyful mysteries of the rosary for the sanctity of your married life. God bless you my daughter.

The day has passed almost unbeknownst to me. Jenny took her lunch to school. The hour has changed for summer-time, the evenings are stretching as fast as myself. That makes sense. I go out into the garden and sniff the dusky air, the ripening year. Progress. It is working away inside me too, working against the dark. Someone comes out of the porchway into the next-door garden. We nod pleasantries over the hedge. I'm not the only one who hopes that things aren't so terrible. Well, if my ankles get more swollen I'll spend all my mornings in bed.

Eleven and a quarter punts. You wouldn't get far on that with swollen pins. No point in asking the travel agent for brochures. You couldn't even afford a day at the seaside, my darling. You won't go wild again in a hurry. Out to lunch with Edna and Company, that's about the size of it. It's not even enough to cover the trainfare for one trip to Dublin. I had to juggle the housekeeping money to make myself available for Leo.

It was then that the famous Noelle myth came into the picture. She was a great deal more useful than other, fickle, pillars of my life. 'Imagine recognising each other after all these years,' Edna marvelled when I described how Noelle and I had bumped into each other in the tweed department at the Kilkenny Design Shop. I described the yellow and orange flecks in the heather-coloured fabric, told how Noelle had a little woman who ran up marvellous suits.

'I never remember any Noelle,' Robin said. 'Do you mean you don't believe me?' I challenged. We had haggled over the words 'disbelief', 'suspicion', 'lack of trust—of faith' so much during the recent months that the term sprang voluntarily from my lips. 'Oh, Jesus Christ!' Robin said.

The following Friday evening Leo ran his hands over my hot bare body. We had a whole night ahead of us and the next day as well, thanks to Noelle. (I never mentioned Noelle's name to Leo.) 'Is this your Sabbath?' I asked. I was feeling grateful and romantic. Leo moved away as if he had been stung by a wasp. We sat up against the pillows for a while. I considered a change of plans, I could leave now and get down to see Bel, get her off my conscience. Then he reached for my hand.

'Noelle was in great form,' I said to Robin when I returned home. 'What did you do?' 'Nothing much, this and that, went into town, lunched in Jury's.' 'That's nice,' Robin said. Looking at it in retrospect, I don't think he was even listening. I could have told him the naked truth and he would just have sat there nodding his head and saying, 'That's nice.'

'Geraldine was asking for you,' Robin says the minute he walks in the door from Killarney.

I hear him, I'm listening. He tries to sound casual but I am perpetually on the lookout.

'She's delighted about the baby. I told her you were blooming.'

When Robin comes over to kiss me I can smell brandy on his breath. I can smell brandy and a faint familiar perfume. We stare at each other impassively, Robin and I. I begin to stroke my belly slowly and deliberately, shifting myself so that he has to be aware of me and my condition, careful to play my cards well.

'Where did you bump into her?' I drawl.

Robin rattles off a few details—the man he was supposed to meet, Geraldine parking her car near his, how he hadn't noticed her until she spoke. All I want is the barest outline. I don't want to know now what I wasn't able to see when it mattered. I don't want to be reminded of Robin's enthralment.

'How did she look?' I ask briskly.

'She has grown thin.'

Geraldine was always thin, it must be because I am so fat, fat with giving life.

'And how is his lordship, Sir Paul?' I manage to make it sound comical.

'I didn't see Paul. I suppose he's alright.' Robin's face is drawn. His eyes have a sleepwalker's stare.

'How is life down in Killarney?' I feel my way cautiously. I don't trust anyone.

'Geraldine says she'll contact you soon,' Robin says.

I smile.

At the time when the whole town was talking about the four of us I overheard someone at a midday cocktail party saying, 'If they're all that friendly it was a bloody funny thing to do.' I wanted to cry but I kept on smiling.

The pilgrimage must continue, you can't turn back.

I ramble into the kitchen and am frightened by the woman in the white nylon coat. She is our new home-help. She is showing Jenny how to make a chocolate mousse. Her name is Mrs Kenny. She is ruddy and snub-nosed, with a jack o' lantern smile. She stirs the mixture with the silver spoon I found in Bel's suitcase. I smother an impulse to snatch it from her, and look instead for the indigestion pills. I don't like this new woman. I don't like the image of myself I find mirrored in her attitude. Her eyes glance off mine like snooker balls.

'The chocolate would have gone mouldy, Mrs King. Poor Jenny likes a pudding. Look—your mummy wants a glass of water!'

Jenny springs to the tap with a tumbler.

Trifle—that's what Bel used to make when I came home for holidays. Big yellow trifles with jam at the bottom.

'It's wonderful that you found someone so capable,' Edna says. She squeezes the slice of lemon into her gin.

We even have slices of lemon. If the day were sunny I'm sure the rims of the glasses would arrive iced and sugared. Even so, I don't like this woman. I lift the lid of the piano and tinkle a few notes which die away as fast as unseasonable butterflies. Edna is hurt— don't I realise that she is sensitive about pianos?

After Edna has gone I walk through the dining-room, pushing chairs out of line. I go up to the bathroom. It is fragrant, gleaming. Mrs Kenny still reminds me of cow parsley, springing up in a big white clump where she isn't wanted. I drank that gin too fast—or maybe it is the indigestion pill. I feel as if my gullet is blistered. At least she goes home before tea—I'm talking about Mrs Kenny. With her mackintosh on over the overall. 'It's the white housecoats,' I said to Robin. 'It is like having a keeper.' 'She'll give you time for yourself and the baby,' he replied. Time for what? I have too much time, great big soup bowls full of it. Betty and I muddled along well enough, keeping out of each other's way. I can hardly wait for five o'clock; the happy-hour when the front door shuts and Mrs Kenny's black laced shoes go scrunching down the gravelled path.

In the meantime I creep around my own house like a decrepit tourist, wishing for fine weather so that I can escape out-of-doors. Maybe Robin wants me to become like his mother, lying on a sofa all day long. Typical of the King men to foist something on you that you don't want, and then to hide themselves behind the best intentions. I should have kicked Mr King with those heavy leather brogues. My father would have been amused.

Oh dear, oh dear. By the waters of Babylon ... There are unconfirmed reports of fighting outside Jerusalem.

Lucky Robin boxed up in his office. I wish I had some business worries to distract me.

I begin to see the sense of breakfasting in bed. Make Mrs Kenny traipse up the stairs with trays and maybe she'll leave.

Edna calls. I receive her in my bedroom. Robin's casual jacket hanging on the wardrobe door makes her melancholy. Tony came and collected his clothes while she was out of the house.

'May's lucky. It's a far worse thing than your husband dying,' she says.

I can't think of any consolation so I start to talk about Noelle. 'In Dublin, Noelle has a woman she inherited from her mother-in-law. She's about one hundred and ten years old. She puts plastic sheeting over the carpets after she has hoovered, and Noelle is afraid to take it up. She's a Jewess, I mean the maid. She sings songs in Yiddish and Noelle doesn't know what they mean. She's afraid that they are curses.'

Edna runs a hand over her hair, which badly needs perming. She is wearing a bulky navy anorak which looks as if it should be Tony's. She carries a few groceries in a string bag.

'I'd better go,' she says.

The hoover hums sweetly in the distance. As she moves towards the door I tell her that Robin met Geraldine in Killarney. I am disappointed, she doesn't even observe the decencies, doesn't show the slightest interest. It seems that Geraldine was just a nine-day wonder.

She dawdles with her hand on the knob, asking, 'Angel, did you ever feel like murdering someone?'

I want to kill *her. And* I wanted to kill Robin when he told me about meeting Geraldine. He can't play the errant husband with me now, all that is past and done with.

If it had been anyone but Geraldine. 'Judas! Judas!' I screamed, terrified. And then the real fatality happened. 'I believe you are well acquainted with the deceased youth's family,' the guard said, licking his thumb. 'Deceased youth'—everything shifted into place, everything shattered. It was no wayward impulse that drove me to respond to Leo's advances. It was either that or a complete shutdown. I was like one of those women in folklore who, possessed by some unaccountable compulsion, disappear for a night or two with the fairies, and have to be burned as witches afterwards.

Everything that has happened to me since seems to be happening to someone else.

Chapter Twelve

It is April Fool's Day and Good Friday as well—what a combination. I can't tell whether it is a joke or a crucifixion, and it is going to be a cold wet Easter.

I don't care. This morning the telephone rang and Ray's voice came bouncing over the wires as clearly as if he was in the next room. Nancy's tea-leaves were correct, except that we must send him enough money to buy his ticket home.

I always knew—the way I always know that hijacking won't happen to me, or that the one that may happen won't succeed, not even if the pilot is killed and thrown down a plastic chute onto the runway—that Ray would come back safely.

'Do you want a pilot? Signal then for Jesus.' Geraldine had a marvellous selection of Protestant choruses which she used to ham-up at parties.

Do you want a pilot? Let him come aboard.

For he will safely guide you across the ocean wide,

Until you reach at last that heavenly harbour.

I'm singing this one as I open Ray's bedroom window to air the place. My happiness is so palpable that I can feel it and smell it, pleasurable as an orange.

'Ray should be able to find his own fare home,' Robin said. His criticism had no effect.. Robin should be pleased. He must be pleased. Ray must be sent money. My fingers itch to touch my son, I won't be denied.

We should be glad that he wants to come home after everything. Look at the troubles other people have. We buried Albert last Saturday and May doesn't know what to do with herself. 'What will become of me?' I heard her say it myself. Tony and Edna sat on opposite sides of the church at the funeral.

Why can't he hitch-hike home?' Robin asked. How could Ray

hitch-hike from Israel? Answer me that. Ray and Don always hitch-hiked together.

I'm appalled by Robin's meanness. I go out in a flurry to see what I can raise from my own skimpy account. It is early, but I want to get it fixed up as quickly as I can. Even though I have only a hundred pounds or so, I'll think of something. But the wooden doors are closed, I might as well hammer at the gates of heaven. And the bank machine in the wall is out of order.

'April Fool,' jeers a cornerboy.

'It's Good Friday, missus,' says his companion.

If I could cut off a limb and send it to Ray I would. If hanging myself on a cross would help I'd do it.

'Even an imbecile knows better than to point a gun at someone,' Robin said in the aftermath of Don's death. It was an unwise remark, it was unfair. Ray's shoulders were too narrow, his voice too shaky as he said, 'Thanks very much.' Israel wasn't my idea, but I could see how it might seem attractive. 'It's not that your dad is against you, it's just that we've all been so upset,' I said. I seemed to be on a perpetual mission between Robin and Ray, patching things over, wrenching promises, rattling myself at them like a Chinese mobile caught in a storm.

Eventually we managed a farewell meal, eaten with subdued goodwill. Just the five of us—Robin, Ray, Jenny, Anne without Brian, myself. Chicken paprika, 'You won't taste chicken like this on the Gaza Strip.' A vulgar joke about a belly-dancer attempted by Jenny. Only now and then a shadow visible at the very edge of vision, 'Will you be allowed to carry a gun?' 'I don't know. I don't expect so.' Just now and then a moment or two of bewitched silence.

And finally, when we had reached a stage of repleted easiness, Leo's name. 'Oh, Mr Abrahamson was asking how you were, Mum.' I glanced at Robin. He was dreamily eating his chocolate mousse. The girls were looking bored. We had drunk several bottles of wine. I didn't give a damn about Leo one way or the other. All that concerned me was Ray, grown thin and pale as a sickle moon. 'He's a nice man, isn't he?' Ray said. 'Very,' I said. I had no reason to feel guilty. 'I'll be meeting his wife in Jerusalem,'

Ray said. I had no reason to be jealous, Leo and I had no claims on each other. This was where I belonged.

'Ray's coming home,' I call to Jenny when I get back to the house. She and Mrs Kenny are in the kitchen. I can hear them laughing.

'Goody, goody, goody,' Jenny says in a dolly chant. She is ironing a pair of jeans. 'Do you hear that, Mrs Kenny? My big, bad, wicked brother is coming home.' She stops and looks sideways at me, then bends her head and irons as hard as she can, as if she knows she has vexed me.

I want to slap her. I want her to sing, and dance around the kitchen, I want her to mirror my insistent joy.

'And if Ray comes home, what's he going to do with himself?' Robin asked. A sensible question. 'Doss around here at my expense?'

He is worse than our bank manager. Once upon a time we had Albert as our bank manager, but now he's no more and there is this fellow with a tweed sports jacket the colour of sick. He rides a bicycle and goes to places like Fatima or Lourdes for his holidays.

'So your son is out in the Holy Land, Mrs King,' the bank manager says. His face is the yellow of an uncooked fish finger. He is just about to leave. His bicycle's safety chain is slung like a scarf around his neck.

'Israel,' I say.

'Ah, yes!' he runs his finger down the column of figures. He has a habit of sucking at his teeth. 'You'd better talk it over with your husband.' Suck, suck. 'Can't get any more out of this one. I'm sorry.' He smiles and sucks. 'What is your son planning to do now?'

I know, thousands out of work and the only time Ray ever earned any money was as a disc jockey in a club. Weekends only, coming in at all hours. 'Don was with me.' That's what he always said.

'What are you depressed about?' Edna says. 'Do you know that on Good Friday I never, even once, went down to the church. What's the point? Tony isn't going to come back.'

'It was April Fool's Day as well,' I say.

'Every day is April Fool's for me. Tony had a boil on his neck at Albert's funeral. I was delighted. I feel so bitchy I must be on the change. Or else it's withdrawal symptoms. I don't take the pill now that Tony isn't here. Did you hear what happened to Doreen's girl?' Edna is so uptight that she can't talk unless she walks around the room at the same time.

My visit to the bank manager becomes a lunatic excursion in the retelling. Edna mops away her laughter, then gets morose again. She is flat broke. Tony has flown off with this piano bird and left her without any sort of allowance. She goes off into a long tra-la-la about how she was so busy worrying about not getting pregnant that she never got round to understanding money matters. She wouldn't have the faintest idea what to say to a bank manager. Tony took care of all the bills. She is going to wear holes in her carpet from walking in circles.

'Look!' An electricity bill rattles in her hand.

I agree, it seems an enormous amount for a lone woman to pay.

'Women have to pay for everything—isn't it true, Angel?'

I nod my head.

'You were right, Angel. A late baby is often good for a marriage.'

I don't reply.

'What does Noelle think? Would Noelle agree?'

'Listen, I haven't met Noelle for months. I don't even know if her father is still alive. That's how out of touch I am.'

That reminds Edna that she can't even spare the money to buy a newspaper, so she has no way of reading the death notices. Doreen had to call round to tell her about Albert.

I pop into the butcher's on the way home. Five pounds in money for a few loin chops. 'How about the oxtail, or sheeps' hearts?'

'They're all booked. It's the recession, missus.'

But I'm not receding, I'm eating for two. Another few punts won't make much difference. 'We can ask the computer, just to satisfy ourselves,' the bank manager said.

Of course I can ask Robin for money. He's a generous man. Twenty, thirty pounds. As long as it's not for Ray's ticket. 'Two twenties. They are for the baby stuff,' I said.

Anne and Jenny come with me. It is Friday night again, another Sabbath, and the shopping centre is packed. Anne and Jenny giggle over the things before putting them into the wire basket—vests, bootees, nighties for the baby.

'And how about this for you, Mama?' Chiffon and swansdown. 'You'd be the real *femme fatale*.'

I throw the nightie back onto the counter. I don't even want to touch the baby garments, they are too unreal, clothes for a pet poodle.

'How would you like to be this size again?'

How would you like to be unborn again?

'How about nappies? What sort of disposables do you want?'

'You two choose.' I go over and look at the displays of bamboo furniture and the imitation plants instead.

By the time we get back home I ache all over, but that's to be expected. I'm lucky to have such big daughters to help me. Daughters old enough to make fresh hamburgers for the family tea while I put my feet up.

'And I have put your pork pieces for tomorrow in the white bowl,' Anne says.

It was Geraldine who gave me my pork pieces recipe, and the one for boiled fruit cake which I never make now. We used to buy all the magazines and wallow in their cookery columns. Sponges for all occasions. Unusual picnics. That sort of thing—*bon appetit!*

Anne must go. She is meeting Brian in the city. The hall door bangs behind her. I stand in the hall as wooden as a statue, the sound reverberating in my ears. As wooden as the Madonna with the childlike face who weathers the years on the church bell-tower.

'What's wrong with you?' Jenny asks.

On such a filthy morning there is no point in telling myself that spring is here.

'The rotten beasts,' Nancy sobs on the telephone.

Her flat has been burgled. She sounds hysterical.

'I have some business to do in Dublin anyway, don't worry, I'll be there by this evening,' Robin says and gets into his car and heads off.

I haven't been in Dublin for months.

I haven't shaken out my glad rags for a party or a dance since I don't know when. I'm frozen as I walk around town because I have put on my peep-toe summer shoes in an effort at gaiety. Everyone examines my feet. My feet or my belly as I stagger, hunted and haunted, from shop to shop. The evenings are brightening and stretching, but I hate this damn cold.

I take some invitation cards out of our writing bureau. Suppose I wrote to Geraldine, pressed her to be godmother—promised a whale of a christening party. She'd have to come.

Most of those parties in Geraldine's house were messy hilarious affairs, with the trees in the garden illuminated by green fairy lanterns, and buckets and buckets of booze. 'You'd want to keep an eye on Robin.' I disregarded the remark. Sometimes, on the spur of the moment, the four of us went off together for a lost day. But Paul and I didn't have much in common, it was Geraldine and Robin who made the running. Or Geraldine and I. It wasn't the usual sort of foursome with the men taking over about business and golf and the women yawning and wishing themselves back at their ironing boards.

I throw the invitation cards into the fire. I'd need a crematorium as big as a bakehouse to destroy everything I'd like to destroy.

Instead I must crouch here in the commandant's house, the house where I have reared his children, waiting for him to arrive with his sister. He won't even lift a finger to help his son return from Israel, his son who is a Gentile to the very core.

I telephone Edna to see if she is in a worse state of mind than myself, but all I get is the engaged signal.

Next morning it is a lovely sunny day. I try Edna's number again. Same thing. Robin and Nancy aren't due until late tonight. I leave the house to Mrs Kenny's ministrations and set out on foot for Edna's. It is sunny but windy, dustbins are out waiting for the binmen, blown-away plastic bags form mock phantoms in the hedges.

Someone has thrown out an old brown suitcase for collection. The name 'Hannah Brady' is stamped on its side. A name that must have belonged to someone, maybe still does, a name that evokes gorse, blossoms, ploughed fields. I pause to examine it, it has the same musty whiff that came from Bel's leavings. A woman comes to the upstairs window of the house and her face frightens me off. Whoever she is, I'll bet she's not poor Hannah.

'There's no one inside,' a gardener tells me. He is digging in the garden next to Edna's.

I have been knocking and ringing for about ten minutes. All the curtains are drawn but a bowl of fresh-looking primroses stands on the downstairs windowsill.

I feel disappointed. I feel cheated of a commiserative chat.

And then I shout with laughter because there is nothing to talk about. It is all lies. If I extricated my family's and stupid friends' heads from the sand they'd peck me to pieces and then scream 'Revolting! Disgusting!' And as for Robin in particular—I haven't been wronged or raped. I'm not going to wreck my marriage.

I continue walking until I reach the centre of the city. There, in a steamy café, I drink a cup of tea. I'm a middle-aged frump, not an Aphrodite, I can't do anything but stay quiet. I'm not the sort of woman that Bel was in her heyday, not giving a tuppenny damn about the neighbours. I'm a very private person.

CHAPTER THIRTEEN

The programme continues according to Mother Nature's plan. I book my room in the nursing home. 'Is it yourself Mrs King? Lovely to see you after all this time.' Matron brings me into her own private den and sits me on a hard chair. She has been expecting me. There are biscuits on a plate, a glass of sherry. She has seen me on the street, people have mentioned my name.

'Who for instance?'

'May, at the flower club, for one. You're Dr Black's patient.' She has to put on her glasses to write it in the book.

Her hair, which was a glistening black beehive when Jenny was born, is sparse and grey. Her legs are bandaged.

She thinks that there is great credit due to me. She moves slowly between the chairs and the fireplace, telling me in her whispery voice of the things she has seen and heard, the way the younger generation behaves. She strokes my hand and pats my hair until I feel suffocated by her presence, her heavy form in its tent-like dress.

'And be sure and give my regards to that lovely man of yours,' she says when I bid her good-morning.

I think of Leo.

'You look like a Madonna,' she says.

Jenny doesn't see me as a Madonna, she sees me as a hulking bore. She can hardly bear to look at me. Instead she gives all her attention to Nancy's burglary. I have heard the details of the break-in so often I know it by heart—how the cushion covers and pillows were slashed, how the floorboards were pulled up in the search for ready money, how the bottle of liqueur from the duty-free airport shop was poured over a patchwork quilt. For me the topic is exhausted, but Nancy starts to cry again at this point.

Robin is out in the greenhouse, setting tomato plants.

I go over and push the television button. The new President of Israel is being interviewed. 'I received my primary education in Alexandra College, Dublin,' he says.

I have an intuition which fades. There is nothing but a whispering, a scuffle out in the hall. When I turn around I am staring at my son.

The things we forget—they rush over me—how thin Ray is, so thin that the white T-shirt sticks to his ribs. It is like having a lost soul in the house. The astonishing strength of his bony fingers. His chewed-down fingernails.

'I still have my door key,' he says, then bypasses other explanations and points at the man on the television screen. 'I've met him,' he says, 'he knew Mr Abrahamson when he lived in Dublin.'

My stomach gives such a lurch that it feels like a labour pain. My happiness is so strong it hurts. Yes it is Ray, complete with rucksack, looking a little strange, appearing so suddenly that it takes an awkward moment for my mind to absorb the fact, my lips to form the word.

It is Jenny who shouts, 'Ray!' before I have uttered a sound, Jenny who rushes over and then halts and grows shy.

'We got in about six o'clock,' Ray says. 'We had something to eat in a chipper.'

My son, I keep thinking idiotically, my son, my son.

Someone turns off the President of Israel. I'm like a film fan watching a thriller. I manage to croak his name as a small anxious girl who looks dead tired appears around the frame of the door.

'This is Hannah,' Ray announces.

Hannah comes over and shakes hands with fingers that feel as brittle as shells. Robin walks into the room and it all starts to happen again.

'Hi, Dad!'

'Who's this?'

'Hallo, Mr King. My name is Hannah Komeskie.'

'Hannah is doing some research. We're travelling together,' Ray says smartly.

And we all pause, overwhelmed by the number of things that we don't know. I'm not the only one who feels out of my depth.

Nancy stands up and says, 'Well, I feel I'm in the way,' and ducks out of the room.

'Where is Nancy going?' Robin asks stupidly.

Then the five of us continue to stand awkwardly silent, like five ghosts struggling with their shrouds. Who is the girl? One of the chosen people I suppose.

'Why didn't you let us know you were coming?' Robin asks.

'Gee, Dad,' Ray rubs his forehead with his knuckles, 'it was just that Hannah had the money. We've been travelling for days. We're still disorientated.'

'There was a terrible fog,' the girl says. Her English is clear and careful.

'This is Hannah's first time in Ireland,' Ray says.

'I'm sorry that we had no opportunity to inform you of our arrival,' she says.

'We read the papers coming over on the ferry. All they seem to be writing about is abortions,' Ray says. Ever since he came in he has been staring at my swelling stomach the way a small child stares at a hedgehog, inquisitively, apprehensively. 'What's happening here?' he asks.

'You can see we don't mind the papers in this house,' I try to sound airy.

'Irishwomen are different I think,' Hannah says seriously.

Different from what?

'Gee . . .' Ray says, and that's all.

I stand there feeling as wobbly as a statue on a pedestal that has just been hit by a wild tennis ball.

'Gee!' Hannah's velvety eyes are also fixed on my shape.

I lick my lips and taste salt, perhaps I'm dissolving in tears. Everything keeps changing colour. Suddenly I hurl myself at Ray, at the girl, words spilling out like champagne bubbles.

The girl makes some mention of the youth hostel, but I brush it aside, press her to stay. We have lots of room, she can share with Jenny, share with Nancy.

'Perhaps it would be better for me to share with Ray, that is if you don't mind, Mr King, Mrs King,' the girl, Hannah, says.

She is a very delicate, swanlike girl, with soft heavy lips. I can't imagine her working in fields or clearing scrubland.

Robin gives a gargantuan sigh. Ray murmurs something I can't catch. Jenny giggles and asks how long has Hannah been in a kibbutz.

'For one year. I was taking care of the smallest ones,' she says.

Ray puts his arm around her.

Very well, if that's what they want—I'm so heady from excitement I can't think straight. 'There's only a single bed,' I'm saying stupidly.

'Oh, we have our sleeping bags—both of us,' she says easily.

'What are you blaming me for?' I cry out when Robin and I are in our own bedroom. 'You wouldn't even give the boy his fare home,' I say, and experience a wicked delight when Robin hides his face in his hands. 'It's perfectly normal,' I say, 'I don't know why you're objecting.'

'What about Jenny—and Nancy?' Robin asks.

'What about Don and Ray when you were philandering with Geraldine?' I throw back. 'What about that—you beast?'

'They didn't know,' Robin says sullenly.

'Everyone knew,' I shout. 'Everyone from Anne and Ray to the man in the moon.'

I have to sit down on a stool. The baby is leaping around, having a party all on its own. The sound of a door banging violently makes Robin and me jump.

'Please,' Robin reaches out a hand, 'please.'

I'm all muddled. I hate this, I hate having that girl in Ray's room. I'm the stickler, I was the one who laid down the rules concerning Anne and Brian, I was the one who insisted that he must never enter our house.

'We can talk about it tomorrow. They've probably been sleeping together for months,' Robin says.

We flop into bed, where I wallow in an ecstasy of weariness.

Robin suddenly embraces me in the dark. 'I'm sorry Angel,' he says. 'It's all my fault about everything.'

I let him hold me, I let him do whatever he wants to do. I feel that we are both roaring downwards in a bottomless pit.

Is it possible to be a martyr without being aware of the fact, or do you have to make the decision yourself? Robin and Ray talk in the sitting-room while I sit upstairs doodling naughts and crosses on an envelope, and thinking, against my will, about Bel's last days.

'What's the rush?' Ray asked when Robin suggested that Hannah should now leave the house. She didn't seem to have any place to go and so we let the matter drop. We're not mad dogs, we're a collection of people trying to behave as correctly as possible in trying times.

Even so, sometime in the middle of the night Robin switches on the bedside lamp and we have a short fierce argument, during which we fling ourselves about like maniacs closed up together in a padded cell. Robin looks drawn and persecuted in the dim glow, his stripy pyjamas remind me of the clothes that convicts once had to wear. I win every time, we have to consider the baby. It serves you right, I think when Robin goes back to his side of the bed and twists about as if he was lying on thorns.

Hannah speaks very good English. I have managed to get half of my breakfast eaten—one slice of toast—and here she is knocking at the hall door with a newspaper under her arm. She left the house before I came downstairs. She always, if possible, starts off her morning by taking a good walk. She is able to find her way around easily by taking note of the various church spires. She is interested in the Irish situation, and she wants the big names identified. She pores over the many letters in the *Irish Times* about the pending abortion referendum. If it is passed, and the new clause inserted in the Irish Constitution, no woman, under any circumstances, will be able to have an abortion in this country—not that they can at the moment anyway.

Hannah says, 'In Ireland they take a tragic view of women, I think.'

I tell her how I had seen, thrown out on the footpath, a brown suitcase with the name 'Hannah' stamped on it.

'But it was not mine,' she says pedantically.

Ray has still not made his appearance, Jenny is dashing off to school, Robin comes, briefcase in hand, and gives me a cool morning-peck on the cheek.

And while Ray is still in bed May calls. She is dressed in black and looking like a typical Irish widow from an earlier period. Hannah studies her curiously. Albert is mentioned with every breath. It is so long since we have met that I even shake hands.

May looks nonplussed as she answers my question about her health. 'Since poor Albert went, as well as could be expected. But I haven't called about myself. It's Edna, she's . . .' May taps her head and looks significant. 'Of course Albert always suspected that.'

Poor, poor Edna. I'm almost ready to weep. 'Ray has arrived,' I say, 'And this is a friend of his.'

You wouldn't believe the questions that May asks Hannah, starting with what did she have for her breakfast. 'You must bring Ray around to visit me, since my husband died I'm very lonely. The boys would be thrilled,' May says.

Somehow, she gets the girl to talk about herself. Hannah, it seems, comes from an aristocratic Portuguese family. Yes, she finds our houses strange, but that is after the kibbutzzïm and not because of the marble floors and huge carved furniture in her own home.

'And you are doing a line with Ray. I mean, you are Ray's girlfriend. Albert would have been tickled pink,' May says.

'I know him from the kibbutz,' Hannah says. She seems irritated.

I gulp down some of the lukewarm tea left in the teapot. The kitchen seems too small and square, the cosiness a sham.

I can't see this Hannah playing an important part in Ray's life. She'll be an episode, brief and comic as a cartoon film. So I console myself as I plod around the supermarket wearing an old fur-lined mackintosh. The weather is filthy for April. Nancy follows me along the lines of shelves, getting in my way.

'She contacted her people in Lisbon today, I believe. They're lonely in their castle without her—as you can imagine,' I say.

Nancy is all dolled up. As usual she is as quick as a bright bird with a grey crest—until someone mentions robbery, then she languishes. She isn't languishing now though. 'I wouldn't keep her under my roof,' she says.

I block my ears and concentrate on the half-price fruit basket, bruised lemons, shrivelled oranges. At least Robin has our tomatoes planted. Be thankful for small mercies, I tell myself, as my woolly cap slips from my head. I don't want to be bothered by Nancy's insinuations. I know that Hannah is female and Ray *vice versa*. I have no idea what they are up to behind Ray's closed bedroom door, but of course I can guess. I pick up the cap and stuff it into my pocket.

I'd be just as glad to tell Nancy to go packing as to tell Hannah. But, 'Remember Nancy helped us out when you had flu,' Robin said. She did like hell. She pushed Betty—who had been our cleaning woman for years—out the door and left me stuck with Mrs Kenny, whom I can't stand. Mrs Kenny with a sneer on her face, nudging Jenny, whispering, 'That one's like something you'd see at a disco,' when Hannah appears complete with Star of David earrings and definitely no bra beneath her white shirt.

'That's flying in God's face,' Nancy says when I say I don't care what Ray and Hannah are up to.

'I'm just glad to have him home. Make love not war, God hasn't got a face,' I say, and leave her to cart the box of food out to the car.

Anne arrives, wearing a piqué blouse as crisp and white as a sheet in an advertisement, just as we are all having a brunch-type meal in the kitchen. 'It's like a documentary on togetherness,' she says, and kisses everyone except Hannah and Mrs Kenny.

'Bring Hannah to the pub tonight,' she says to Ray.

Then the kitchen empties and I am left with a pile of dirty dishes as big as a tombstone and Mrs Kenny has gone home. And it looks as if I'll have to get in more provisions in spite of the fact that I spent a fortune on food this morning. The baby is moving all the time. I wish I could go to bed and sleep for three months and wake up at the end of July and start afresh.

And the weather is miserable, miserable. The worst April in over sixty years—that's before anyone in this house was born. Pale sun and black scudding clouds play hare-and-hounds across the sky.

'You and I could go away for the weekend if you like,' Robin suggests, even though it is pouring rain. We haven't seen sunshine since Ray came home.

'No thanks,' I say.

Upstairs, I step delicately across the carpet in Ray's room. The two sleeping bags are on the floor, the bed is also rumpled. I don't go near it. And I keep out of Nancy's way because she has me badgered. 'How long is that girl going to stay here?' 'What plans has Ray for the future?' An empty beer bottle sticks out of Hannah's rucksack. I open the window to let in some fresh air. Next thing they know, I'll be up in the nut-house with Edna.

I glare at the dining-table. We have run out of mustard. Ham salads and no mustard, and I'd forgotten Hannah won't eat the meat of the pig. Won't eat meat, period. She's a vegetarian.

My car doesn't stop at the shop but keeps on moving out the road, on and on until I'm driving along witchy twisty lanes in County Clare. A narrow road, punctuated with graveyards, graveyards full of Celtic crosses which are the only sign that human life was ever here. Water runs in rivulets down into the ditches as if the fields are being squeezed like sponges. The bedraggled banks are clogged with clump after clump of drowning primroses. There is nothing alive except myself, and a rabbit that goes bobbing along the road in front of the car. Excuse me—I forgot the child rolling so energetically in my womb.

At last I get home and here is Jenny, out in a yellow mackintosh and huge orange cowboy boots, yelling at my car. They have been searching everywhere, were even getting ready to telephone the guards. Jenny refuses to be pacified although I think I deserve congratulations for finding my way home at all.

'There's no need for a big scene,' I keep begging while everyone makes a commotion.

'We thought of everything,' Anne says, 'Dad even came out to the cottage.'

'We thought—'

'It's alright. She's home safe,' Robin interrupts.

It seems that I have arrived just in time to prevent them from raising a general alarm. Anne has heated soup and they all stand watching me while I drink it.

'You'll know me the next time you see me,' I say to Hannah, who becomes embarrassed and tugs Ray over to sit on the sofa.

Nancy makes a stab at light conversation. 'I told them you wouldn't have taken the mink if you were going to do anything silly.' Her high tra-la-la of phoney amusement dies on her lips.

I examine myself. I am wearing my mink, it is soaking wet. I must bear a striking resemblance to a cornered baboon. No wonder they all look frightened.

'You've been gone for five hours,' Robin says.

'I went for a drive and lost my bearings,' I reply.

'In this weather!'

Anne takes away my mug and helps me out of my wet fur. I realise what a spectacle I must be, as disreputable and awkward as a pantomime dame. I don't know how to account for myself. I am heavy with child, that must excuse everything.

'How did you get so wet? Why didn't you take cover?' Robin is asking.

We stare at my squelching shoes, my swollen ankles. They are all as bewildered as I am.

'Well then, if everything is alright, I'll head off,' Anne says brightly.

She sets the pattern for the others. Ray and Hannah, Jenny, Nancy, they all trot out pat excuses, they all have jobs to do. Robin and I are left on our own.

'You're all in one piece anyway,' Robin says with fake heartiness when the silence becomes nerve-racking.

I'm in two pieces, that's the trouble.

Robin looks as white as a sheet.

'I couldn't find any signposts. All the roads look the same,' I say.

It has been as wet today as any day earlier in the year, even as wet as that January day when I travelled to Dublin and tried to see Leo. That terrible afternoon, that fiasco. This time I had been sure, as I tried to find my way back along those country roads, with everything blurring in the rain, that I would never get back.

Robin brings a towel, kneels down and takes off my sopping shoes. There is a tacit agreement that we won't quarrel tonight.

CHAPTER FOURTEEN

'The foetus is the baba throbbing in the womb of the mama and very much alive,' the Monsignor says.

I am a big heap sitting uncomfortably on the church bench beside Robin and the baba is throbbing like crazy.

'You'll be bringing forth children yourself,' Father Bussey said to me during that dreadful time so long ago when my father died. I suppose he was trying to console me.

May is sitting in front of us, flanked by her sons. And in the same seat with her is Francesca, and Francesca's husband, and Francesca's baby who looks over Francesca's shoulder at us with forget-me-not eyes.

'She went to Punchestown for the races,' Bel used to say when a girl in the town whom everyone knew was pregnant went off to visit an aunt and came back as thin as a herring.

May is hanging on the Monsignor's every sentence, nodding her head at the punch lines. For myself, I can take it or leave it. What do plump worthy men know about having a stranger's baby? But May is heavily involved these days in the local campaign in support of the Government's plan to make abortion under any circumstances impossible. Francesca's infant pulls a fierce face and begins to bellow. The Monsignor stops in mid-sentence and doesn't resume until Francesca's red-faced husband has taken the child and gone charging out of the church.

'In the case of this baba . . .' the Monsignor resumes. ' . . . Our Blessed Lady, God's own mother . . .'

She sure had a stranger's baby. Holy Mother of God, I pray. Let me hang on and we'll go and have a drink down the road before I return home to finish the dinner.

'I don't do much socialising these days,' May says.

Robin, in a flush of neighbourliness, has insisted that she come down to the hotel with us for a drink. Francesca and the others have plans elsewhere.

'I must show you these.' May produces a wallet full of photographs taken at Albert's grave on the day after his funeral.

I can't think of any comment except, 'The flowers are marvellous, the flowers are marvellous,' over and over again.

Robin just grunts, but I feel a sentimental twinge about Albert, remembering him trying to embrace me down by the lake when he was on his last legs. Poor sod.

May has too much make-up on her face, a thick layer all over the bags and wrinkles, which makes her skin look like that of an inferior peach and leaves a film of dust around the collar of her dark wool suit.

'I've got rid of the big car at last,' she says. Albert hadn't driven it for more than a year, but for as long as he was alive it had remained in their driveway. 'It's great to see the pair of you looking so well,' she says, sitting with her feet sturdily planked on the carpet and smiling a brave smile. 'It's couples like you who give the good example. Francesca says she won't have any more babies.'

Robin won't hear of May buying us a drink and so she gives us badges to wear which signify that we believe unborn children have equal rights with the rest of us.

'Is Ray still with you?' she says when we gather our things to leave.

In the carpark she climbs into her old Morris Minor and, because she is a bad driver, we give her time to pull out and get away ahead of us. When we drive out onto the road there's May with her car stalled beneath the chestnut trees. We stop to see if she's alright and she starts bawling, louder and fiercer than her grandchild did during Monsignor's sermon. Great gobbets of tears that must have been accumulating for weeks spurt down her cheeks.

'You don't know, Angel,' she says to me when I open the passenger's door, 'you can't understand. You have Robin.'

I perform absurd contortions trying to fit myself into the car beside her while Robin bumbles platitudes through the window.

'The first year is the worst, May.'

I don't know who told me that. The first year is horrific. . . They could have been talking about babies and not bereavement. I sit there, squashed in on top of May, feeling sad and frightened at the chancy quality of everything, while May's hand lies cold and dead as a landed fish on my burning palm.

My mink coat has gone into cold storage. That is the only sign of impending summer.

'You look wonderful,' Doreen says. She speaks in an affected hoity-toity voice.

We are standing between the shelves in the library and I can smell brandy on her breath. I came up here to escape from everyone but it obviously can't be done.

'What would you recommend, Angel?' she asks. 'Nothing heavy, please.' Her face is drawn and thin. 'Why don't you call around sometime?'

I don't want to involve myself. I don't want to ask about the child with the drug problem. I pat her shoulder and leave her poking through the shelves. I make my own choice in record time. I want to get away quickly, but Doreen follows me out to the library door. Torrential rain is falling and I am trapped.

'Have you seen May lately? I can't get used to meeting her without poor Albert.'

It is raining so hard that the water running down the channels froths like the head on pints of stout. There is not another soul in sight.

'Have you picked a name for the baby?' Her eyes are enlarged by her reading glasses and she has unhealthy pink patches on her cheeks.

I am not imagining the brandy. More Guinness goes chortling down the drains, it's a real rain-stopped-play day. No, I haven't given a thought to naming this child. I jangle my car keys to cover up the silence. Doreen looks at me in a shifty way, as if she is the one who is trying to keep a secret. When she hiccups I want to laugh. I don't mind what she does, she can drink her head off if she likes. May, Edna and Doreen, that makes three of my acquaintances who are in varying degrees of bad shape.

'I might call her Noelle after my friend in Dublin,' I say.

'And supposing it's a boy?' Doreen has recovered herself. 'Will you call him after his dad?'

'As long as it's healthy.' I go over and lean against the wall. She is not going to grind me down with the facts of life.

'I know. At your age,' she jumps in.

But I refuse to be bothered, I refuse to be troubled. Even so, I suddenly feel sick and so dizzy that she has to find me a chair. So here I am, stuck in the dismal hall, staring at a poster advertising painting holidays in the Burren. Doreen and the attendants swarm around me, asking me if I want to go to the hospital.

Jenny is coming down the wooden stairs from the reference library wearing that horrible second-hand battle jacket which I ordered her to throw away. Oh, this is great, this is the comforting thing about offspring—the marvellous way they step over their mothers' ailing bodies and out into the wide-wet world. And the fellow that Jenny is with looks dangerous. He even has a big swastika printed on the back of his leather jacket. I watch him dash across the street with Jenny, and wince at the cigarette butt which she tosses onto the wet road.

'That pair,' one of the attendants says, 'we'll have to start charging them rent. It has been going on for the past month.' She and the other girl giggle.

'Was that Jenny?' Doreen asks.

I don't reply. I'm sure I'm purple with rage. Even so, the dizziness has passed.

And here's a man with a large, long, pale whiskery face poking his nose in. 'What's wrong with the lady?' he wants to know.

I recognise this old gent. He is one of the local pests. He has been following me for years, annoying me with his bullock's notions. But any port in a storm. However, his attention is fixed on Doreen. I can see her uncurling under his attention. She is talking too much, too loudly and too fast.

'The city's most regal beauty,' he says, and kisses her hand. He carries a book of poetry. He recites some verses he claims to have written himself.

The rain has eased and Doreen says she will see me to my car.

The man clutches his plastic mac and sighs, 'I wish I could lie with you tonight. No offence, madam, I hope.'

'I suppose he's harmless,' she says as we scurry down the road. She hiccups and this time doesn't even apologise.

He is about as dangerous as a swastika on a teenage layabout's jacket.

Instead of going straight home I call to Billy Black's consulting rooms. Nothing serious, I'm just not feeling too well, nausea, light-headedness.

'What do you expect at your age?' Billy asks.

'I don't want this baby,' I say.

Billy Black thinks that this is another big joke. 'Wait until it's born and then you'll find you have a soft spot for it,' he says.

I'm beginning to feel that I have absorbed so much—not just Leo's sperm, but everything else in this crazy world as well—that I'll explode.

It is the first week in May. Two more months before the baby. Even walking as far as the garden gate costs me an effort, but I force myself to make plans, keep going.

I visit Edna. She has been taken into hospital for treatment for her nerves. She wears an awful red dressing-gown and huddles in a chair beside a big window which gives a view of a stone wall. She falls asleep while I am telling her about the traffic-jam in William Street. I don't like to leave her there, sleeping. She looks as if she might topple over and hit her head on the old-fashioned radiator. When I shake her awake she clasps my wrist with eager fingers and makes me promise to bring her in a nail-file as soon as possible. I agree, but coming out of the hospital I begin to worry, and soon convince myself that a nail-file might be counted as a dangerous weapon. (A young man who worked with Robin became ill and persuaded a friend to bring him in a packet of razor blades.) I go to a chemist and buy a packet of emery boards.

I've decided that the time has come to buy equipment for the baby. I make Robin accompany me. We are both appalled at how much everything is going to cost—carry-cot, cot, baby-buggy, high-chair and so on.

The salesman plainly considers us ludicrous. 'No sir, we don't do second-hand lines,' he says to Robin. 'Mummies and daddies don't admire that style of article nowadays, missus,' he says when I ask him to show me a high pram.

'I give up,' Robin mutters to me as he roots for his cheque-book.

He is wearing his new grey suit. He was wearing it yesterday as well. He put it on yesterday morning because he was going to meet a client in Tipperary, it was the first time he had worn it. I pick up the match-book that tumbles onto the counter when he pulls out his cheque-book. As I take in the name of the Killarney hotel I am reminded of the first time I really noticed Robin and Geraldine. They were dancing together and when the music stopped they continued to sway. Then Geraldine lifted her head from Robin's shoulder, saw me, and wriggled her fingers. It took months before the penny dropped. I'm quicker on the uptake nowadays.

'So your client cancelled the appointment and you went to another one down in Killarney! Oh yes, I believe you. Absolutely!'

I suppose that all the lies which husbands tell their wives, and wives tell their husbands, have a certain sameness. Cancelled appointments, chance meetings, oversights, slips of memory, old schoolfriends.

We go to a pub instead of our house. It is as if we need to be on neutral ground. The place is almost empty in the middle of the afternoon, and as dark and damp as a small badly lit aquarium. We have to peer at each other, and keep our voices low because of the two young men drinking at the counter. In another place, another time, they could be Don and Ray.

The glum funeral air, the dampness, the constricted seating area—too small to swing a cat in—the peculiar time of day, increase my sense of urgency. I must know everything, I must be told immediately.

'There is nothing to tell,' Robin says for the umpteenth time.

He must think I'm a dummy. 'You've been seeing her all the time without telling me,' I say.

Robin snorts. 'When? You must think I have seven-league boots.'

I remember the magical quality that had entered our lovemaking at that time, making me feel the luckiest woman in the world after all these years. I had never known Robin so passionate as when he was becoming infatuated with Geraldine. I remember how we managed to make love of a sort the other night, the night that I found my way home in the storm.

'Did you have sex?' I ask sternly.

Robin is transfixed. He begins to pat the pockets of his suit as if he is nervous that all sorts of further incriminating evidence will come tumbling out—condoms, rubber phalluses, sex manuals, spangled tights. It reminds me of a blue movie.

He takes out his car keys. 'Please, Angel,' he says, 'just let it pass.' He puts his hand at the back of my head and pulls it forward until our foreheads are touching. 'We're still together—all of our lives. And now we have this baby coming—isn't that right?'

Right. At this stage of my pregnancy the baby feels as if it is pressing on my lap when I sit down. It terrifies me.

'She'll be passing through here very soon. She'll look you up herself then,' Robin says.

'Geraldine,' I whisper. It is Geraldine who should be having this baby. It is Geraldine who needs a child, I who should be sterile.

'I'm not as big a prick as you make me out to be,' Robin says. 'It was old Billings who got us into this mess. And if you want to know, it is taking as much out of me as it is out of you.'

I'm restive. I want to leave now, get out before I do something hot-headed, like blurting out all my secrets. I don't believe you, Robin, or rather, I don't totally believe you. But it suits me to believe some of it—half-a-loaf is better than a famine. I don't want to end up keeping Edna company. I've got to keep going.

The television blares. I swear that Nancy is never going to go back to her flat and job, but plans to sit out the rest of her life watching rubbish about American heiresses in our front room. She even forgot to take the chicken pie out of the freezer. She's lucky that I don't bash her head in with the frozen slab the way that the woman did in an Alfred Hitchcock mystery play once, killed her husband with a frozen leg of lamb and then thawed it out and fed it to the detectives. No wonder Robin stays out drinking.

'I'm tied hand and foot,' I insist, when he rings and says I must come in and join him.

'Come on, Angel,' Robin coaxes. 'I've got a surprise for you. Honest.'

Even walking into the hotel, I'm in two minds. It's a hotel I haven't been inside for well over a year. I can hear Paul's voice singing 'The Croppy Boy' as I push open the swing door. It's the song he used to sing on the nights after rugby internationals. We didn't go to any matches this year, I'm not even sure if the Triple Crown was won, or how Ireland fared.

'Angel! Angel! We thought you were lost.' Geraldine sees me before the others. It is she who climbs down from her stool and hugs me. 'I've heard your wonderful news,' she says.

She is tipsy and so are Paul and Robin. They must have been here for ages before they phoned me up.

'I wanted to go out to the house, but Robin said no. He made us stay here.' Geraldine nuzzles her nose into my neck.

I had forgotten that *pot-pourri* of perfume and cigarette smoke, the jangle of her charm bracelet. 'Nancy is out in the house. And Ray. Ray is home from Israel, he brought a girlfriend with him,' I say quickly.

'Ray?'

I had forgotten Geraldine's hooded eyes and that catch in her voice.

She steps back and gives me the once-over. 'I've a bone to pick with you, miss,' she says, 'you never wrote and told me all the exciting details, you never let me know about the baby.'

'Robin told you.'

Geraldine nods and my heart twists.

'It happened last autumn,' I add, as if it mattered tuppence when it happened.

'Come here to me, Angel.' Paul insists on pulling me over and giving me a big wet kiss. 'It's good to see you, gorgeous.' He fondles my belly and proclaims I'm a queen on a throne, a fine example of domestic bliss. 'I'll kill this fellow if he's not looking after you properly,' he jostles Robin's elbow.

'Paul . . .' Geraldine's voice flutters between us, as easy as a dove.

'I hope it's twins,' Paul blusters. 'I bloody well hope its twins for the Kings.'

'The Lord deliver us,' Robin shouts, and calls for another round of drinks.

The barmaid starts laying down the law. It is almost closing time.

'I'd like nothing better than twins—except for triplets, you bugger!' At a certain stage in Paul's drinking savagery develops.

When he gets to this phase I'm the person with the most soothing influence. 'Paul!' I get up on the stool next to his and lean forward to stare into his face. He's the same as he always was, exactly the same—cranky but goodhearted.

'Oh—we must behave ourselves. We mustn't shock Angel.' He plucks at the stuff of my current grow-bag.

We were never a triangle, we formed a square, a foursome. It was always a solid set-up, it could have accepted almost anything.

'How are the family?' Paul speaks so low that only I can hear him.

Geraldine is showing Robin a sheet of paper. The bar is closing down.

'Fine.'

'And Ray?' Paul has started massaging my knee, pinching and rubbing it so hard it hurts.

'Ray's alright.'

I keep my knee in the same place, force myself to bear the agony. Paul continues to squeeze and knead. My knee is going to be black and blue tomorrow. I don't want to move, I don't want Paul to lift his head. I'm afraid I'll see tears.

'I'm glad that you're alright, Angel,' he tells me. 'You're what counts. You're the pick of the bunch.'

'I didn't know the gun was loaded'. That was one of the comic songs that Robin and I knew when we were children. And the others, 'Mary Ellen at the church turned up', 'Two lovely black eyes', 'Nursie, come over here and hold my hand'. They keep coming back into my head and I hum them for a while and then they stop.

That's while I'm getting ready to have lunch with Geraldine. Not that there is much to getting ready—a clean blouse under this ghastly pinny, the raincoat on top of everything, flat shoes.

We're going to a new place, a place that has opened since she left town. I nurse her presence here under my heart with the baby. I didn't even mention it to May in the supermarket this morning. I could just see her winkling Geraldine out and getting her to agree that I'm looking wrecked, talking about me behind my back. I'm glad we have a new restaurant to eat in. I couldn't bear the old place, where Ray and Don in their rosetted confirmation suits walloped into chicken and chips.

But, of course, the new place turns out to be a disaster as well, a gimmicky false place with fake milking stools and a jungle of dusty plants on the flagged floor.

'Jesus, I feel gaunt beside you,' Geraldine says, even though she has put on some weight again.

Then the manageress darts out of the shadows, a thin black viper from the old place, with a pussy-cat bow under her chin. She knows Geraldine at once. In fact she lived down the road from Geraldine, and her people and Geraldine's came from the same village.

'How is your sexy husband?' she asks Geraldine. 'Still as handsome as ever?' Up close her face is the same colour as the sawdust on the floor. 'Tell him I want to meet him.' She wags her finger. Then she hurries off with her peculiar gait that makes her look as if she's darting against a strong wind. In seconds she's back to take our order.

When she moves away again Geraldine speaks as fast as she can. 'I'm glad I saw you, Angel. I want you to know Paul and I are splitting up.' Her face is as bland and smooth as the damask tablecloth.

Well, what can you say to that? Especially if you feel as if you've fallen into a boghole. I toy with the earthenware pepper-pot, spinning it round and round between my fingers until it topples over.

'I don't know how I'd have coped without Robin's advice,' she says.

I don't know how I'm supposed to feel, perhaps I'm meant to feel flattered. Perhaps I'm meant to be as understanding as I was when I discovered that my best friend had put her eye on my husband. But I have lost my innocence now. I've been into the black hole myself. Even if I have any objections I have no right to voice them.

'The only reason we came to Limerick is so that I could tell you myself. I asked Robin not to mention it.'

I keep staring at a mousehole—or maybe it's a rat's—in the skirting board near our table. I have a horror of rodents, if I see one at this stage the baby will probably be born with a hideous birthmark.

'Well that's that. Sorry to be dreary, you've got your own affairs,' Geraldine says and starts arranging her cutlery into criss-crosses.

'Yes—except that this isn't Robin's baby that I'm having,' I say.

She drops her dessert spoon with a clatter.

As the food arrives I give her the bare bones of the situation. On the scale of disasters it begins to seem surprisingly small. I can even see the funny side. It's like being let out of prison. Geraldine keeps staring down at her salad as if she expects it to walk away from under her nose.

'You're not just imagining this, Angel?' she interrupts at one stage.

'I had a job coming to terms with it myself,' I say equably as I lift a forkful of poached salmon. It has been wonderful to make a clean breast of things, to share the incubus with her.

'It won't sink in.' She gulps some wine. 'It's not like you, Angel. It's not your style.'

'I don't have to tell you that Robin doesn't suspect anything.'

'Of course not,' she answers quickly, much too quickly.

All sorts of ideas run into my head. 'Did Robin say anything to you?' I ask. I'm trespassing in no-man's land. Get back to suburbia! 'Forget it,' I say, and begin to chatter about Edna, about Nancy, about Bel's funeral. Seeing Geraldine has acted like a tonic. 'I'm finding it hard to survive without you,' I say.

She pours us both more wine. It tastes like paint-stripper.

'Don't start underrating yourself, Angel,' she says, 'I'm certain you're going to outlast us all.'

I begin to feel pleasantly sluggish, a huge soft globe bobbing along on waves of friendship. 'Here's to all of us. Here's to the cuckoo in the nest.' I lift my glass.

'Angel!' Geraldine gives a shout of laughter.

'Well it's only half a cuckoo, it's half mine,' I say.

'Listen pal—yours and Robin's. Three's a crowd don't forget.' She winks at me.

'So why don't you and Paul make it up?' I push. I feel capable of settling everyone's problems.

'We won't argue. It's a different ballgame.' Geraldine begins to collect her belongings, look for her purse. 'One piece of advice,' she offers as we divide up the bill. 'Don't turn this infant into a golden calf. Remember a child is a child is a child. You have yourself to think of first.'

She's the same old Geraldine, dry-eyed to the bitter end. I'm only trotting after her when it comes to guts.

Of course I don't mind if Robin goes fishing, he needs the break, and Nancy has left for Dublin in the wake of Ray and Hannah. She left reluctantly but I didn't give her much of a choice because the decorator is here to put up the nursery wallpaper on the spare-bedroom walls.

Mrs Kenny hasn't turned up. It means that my morning is a mad scramble of beds, fires, kitchen, stew and potato peels. And every other second my body seems to take on a new shape.

Finished, I sit alone on the sheepskin rug. Madam Wolf being serviced by a sheep. I sit there until the telephone rings and it's Doreen with a litany of domestic knickknacks—a child in hospital, broken washing machine, yesterday's visitors, and did I meet Geraldine—she was seen in town—and how is she keeping? I can't tell Doreen what I'll tell Mrs Kenny. I can't say, 'Scram!'

When I put down the receiver I feel lonely and begin to think about Robin. I know Robin is lying. 'Fishing' with his 'sister' I suppose. He and Geraldine in a lakeside cottage, but who cares? The only company I want is the rain pattering on the windowpane. No one could fish in this weather. And Jenny is lying in bed, missing school. She is going to end up a nothing, but that's her affair. I've changed our sheets, set the fire, cleaned the kitchen, cooked a meal.

Coals glow in the grate although I can't remember striking a match. In fact I thought I was walking along the Dublin quays with Leo, arm-in-arm, looking at antiques, furnishing our love-nest.

A letter came from the bank this morning. Robin is *not* financially shaky. This is a bourgeois nightmare.

The clock strikes twelve and the brass bed is an empty cup, the love-seat a crushed cigarette-end.

When I go into Jenny's room she makes a great show of being occupied although I know that the second before I opened the door she was lying on her bed with all the books closed. She doesn't want stew, she says, because she cooked herself a frozen ham pancake. Before that she did her washing, a week's supply of wet panties drip from the bed-end.

'But it's raining!' she says when I tell her to put them on the line in the yard.

Her transistor blares away, and the room is as stuffy and noisy as a chipman's van. A travel poster of Rhodes—blue sky, sunset, ancient buildings—is pasted onto the side of her wardrobe. She has cut up a pretty blue dress I bought her and turned it into lopsided cushion covers. They are embroidered in red thread—hearts, stars, and, on one, a swastika.

'Go away!' Jenny says as my shadow looms over her possessions.

I do. I go for a long walk in the drizzle and meet no one. The front gardens are silent as abandoned graveyards. Big new houses stand empty and unloved.

CHAPTER SIXTEEN

'Even if we were going to do it, the baby would have changed everything. You must know that.' He stands, warming himself beside the kitchen stove.

I can't believe what I'm hearing. I can't manage to take in the fact that he means it.

It seems that he and Geraldine did discuss the prospect seriously.

'But . . .' Robin takes my hand.

There is my belly, rounded and pale as a paper lantern. Here we are posed as solicitously as any pair in an improving tableau. 'Problems of Ireland today', I embody them all. If he thinks he'll be able to ditch me as soon as I'm thin as a rake again he's mistaken.

'Divorce is against the law,' I say.

'Oh, we were going to go to England.'

When he has gone down to the hotel for his lunch I dump the brown paper bag full of fish into the dustbin while the tomcat nuzzles my ankles. My shouts still echo in my ears. The people next door must have thought that there was a riot. 'You are able to live with the fact of Ray and his girlfriend,' Robin said, and then he was off like a shot. I hope they give him roast donkey to eat, or kangaroo.

I'm not going through a crisis, I'm suffering from lack of initiative. I'm a jazz band's big drum. The baby dances under my skin.

. . . I'm flanked by bishops and politicians and I could walk across the pale grey expanse of the River Shannon in perfect safety. . . .

Ooops! I beg your pardon; it's baby's breakfast—one black pudding, one white pudding, a rasher, an egg—that made me belch.

I'm rented property and the lease will soon be up.

I'm building up morale from the inside. I can't see anything but I feel quite a lot. Even while my partner sleeps there is often a flurry.

Now it has stopped. For a second—then threatened chaos.

No fire. No dinner. Who's going to straighten things up? Angel will, instead of dreaming about last autumn and her act of madness.

. . . The bedsprings creak, raindrops beat on the drum and I'm dancing once more. I'm not coming out in this stormy weather. I'm not going to be hooked like a salmon trout and yanked into the miserable light of day just to be thrown in the bin, if not carved up between them. I don't want almonds scattered over me. I don't want instruments poking at my soft pink flesh. I'm not the cheesecake. My curves are in the wrong place. I want to be flat, flat as a board again . . .

It was alright when I was feeling sorry for Robin. He slammed the door as he left the house and I felt as if a forest had fallen . . .

Geraldine and Paul went straight back to Killarney from Limerick, what happens next is their business. They don't have to tell me . . .

If I lie in the foetal position this party mood should go away. I remember how frightened I was when Anne was born. I didn't know about that gush of blood at the very beginning. 'I'm haemorrhaging,' I wept and the nurse shook me. 'That's normal. That's a show.'

'Poor girl!' Robin is back. It is his hand on my forehead, he who pulls down the blinds. 'You should go out and meet May or Doreen,' he says.

I want to stay here in the silence and warmth. I don't much want to see anyone. I'm as easy as a fern in a pot. But I think it is lonelier with a sleeping, silent partner than it is on your own.

I sit there, beady-eyed as a bird on her nest. Another day is on the blink, but I'm not switched off—not yet . . .

I wonder if Leo thinks of me at all. I wonder if Ray will give him the news. Robin and I have never made love in the bath. Geraldine recommended it. I found it gave me goose-pimples. 'Why shouldn't you be foolish now and then?'

'To a darling fool,' Leo wrote on the card that came with the box of chocolates . . .

Birds sing as the dawn rises, little pieces starting off another day. Threads pull households into life. Mother—brother—sister—husband—wife—son—daughter—father. Eight people squashed into an average double bed. What you might call a proper collection all lying very still. We haven't counted the baby. There is very little to be noted except the quietness when the birds have stopped. I'm floating in my fishskin . . .

Never mind the delusions of grandeur, I know myself for a damp squib. And I'm lucky, this is a very mild sort of loneliness . . .

Today live children can be delivered of women already dead. I think that in my case it was undiagnosed toxaemia—my mother had already gone into labour before the doctor was called. Another million marks were entered against my father in her family's black books. She didn't regain consciousness, just lay there while everything cracked in dismay . . .

'Come here,' Leo said. I had looked forward all day to making love, savoured it with every mouthful of sole *bonne femme*. The result, of course, is the usual sort of mish-mash. From such daft moments the world is peopled.

We are all signs of the times of our own conceptions. It bears out how little we consider others. We don't give tuppence who our parents are. All we want is to use them to make our mark. Pain or inconvenience is not considered, death and heartbreak carry no weight.

That's all gobbledygook.

Baby and me. Up it goes, down it goes, in a see-saw arrangement.

But we have got to be realistic. That nursery wallpaper isn't quite the thing and there is an air of frightening orderliness about the room itself. What does Anne think? Anne thinks it's fine. It used to be her room and now she'd like it back.

I haven't seen Anne for ages. Yet here she is, laden with books, clothes, and all her worldly goods. My oldest daughter, my sister.

I hadn't believed in her telephone voice, which cut loose, metallic and sharp, from the black holes.

I don't want to become involved. I'm wrapped up in a perfect relationship—mother and unborn child. What both of us want is a good holiday. I put my arm around Anne's shoulders. Her relationship with Brian is terrible, she has become a second-class citizen. It is all very dramatic. It demands breakfast trays and a log-book. A cheering cup of tea and, 'Day one, this happened . . .'

'Wait until you're married as long as myself and your father.'

'You and Dada . . . that's different.'

My heart goes out to her. The whole project is quite useless. I arrange Robin's discarded clothes on a hanger, his gardener's clothes. I feel harried and gloomy. Bel had a Spanish shawl which she used to throw over the muddled heaps of garments on the horsehair sofa. I swore I'd be tidy when I had a house of my own.

I wish my mind wasn't such a wrung-out sponge.

'I'm Bridget . . .'

I give it another squeeze, but it is dry as a bone.

'Sorry?'

'Anne's friend. I heard . . .'

I won't even apologise. I'm like someone who has been missing for months. I can't put things in their place anymore. My whole existence is geared towards the coming event. It's not worthwhile remembering the past.

'We can't go on like this,' Robin starts saying.

He is so worried about everything that he has developed a psychosomatic rash on his legs and his stomach. He scratches it in his sleep and I wallop him until he wakes up. He is extremely pessimistic. He has taken to putting bandages on his hands before he goes to bed. He reminds me of a boxer between bouts—I'm not throwing in the towel, I'm not giving up.

'Did Ray call into Leo Abrahamson's office?' he demands of me. Some arrangement had been made about an appointment, there was a prospect of a reasonably steady job.

'How would I know? I'm not even sure where Leo's office is.'

Robin's eyes are crazed and bloodshot. He appears at my side of the bed like an obsequious flunkey, a venomous butler carrying the sleeping pills that Billy Black said I must take, and a glass of water. 'I thought you told me you met Leo outside his office when you were up visiting that woman you went to school with.'

I used to be able to read his mind. I used to have a pretty good idea of what he was thinking. 'You're beginning to sound like Paul,' I say. (Paul used to be obsessive about Geraldine's actions—who had she met, what had she seen, how many people were there, marathon enquiries.) I take my pill and swallow it.

'I've just been doing some minor research,' Robin says. He starts to wind the bandages around his fingers with a pitiful air.

'On me!' I'm prepared to hit back, give no quarter.

'On Ray. He never went near Leo.' He holds out his hands with their dangling dressings, waiting for me to tie the knots. His pyjamas are open, his pot belly a dimly flushed echo of mine. 'Leo can't do anything for him now, he's off to San Francisco for a month—to a conference.'

I think of all the San Francisco women with their candy-floss hair, girls with long legs, and waistlines, waiting to couple with Leo. A whole city of Leo fans, new lamps for old *ad infinitum*.

'You've tied them too tight,' he says.

I hold my tongue as I unloosen the knots, but then I have to find out. 'Did Leo ask for me?'

'Oh—no—no. I was Leo's secretary I spoke to,' he says.

'Miss Cherry Log,' I say.

'Who?—I damn well hope he is short of cash.'

'Who—Leo?'

'Ray!'

'I'm tired.' I give an appropriate yawn and lie down.

I am woken again after an hour or so by Robin's fierce scratching. He must have been down to the lavatory. The bandages are thrown on top of the blankets. I think what a suitable rope they would make. I'm gone beyond caring about any man. I allow myself a few moments of voluptuous sadism—on Robin, on Leo—before I start to thump.

'They're looking for the woman of the house,' Robin says.

It's more canvassers, two women—one in tweed, the other

wearing a black velvet jacket and bright pantaloons—asking for a vote for a woman's right to choose.

'At least you won't be lonely,' the tweed woman nods sympathetically at my bulge. She has a wild nest of white hair and eyes as blue as a newborn infant's.

'I don't know the suburbs. Is there any point in trying across the road?' pantaloons asks.

None at all. There's a big house of priests and next to it a women's hostel run by nuns.

Pantaloons has a series of brilliant scarves entwined with gold chains. The effect is very stylish.

'You might like one of these. We're having a poetry reading to raise funds.' Tweed suit hands me a pink sheet of printed paper, another glider.

'Sunday morning. Do you more good than going to church,' pantaloons says.

Then we stand there, the three of us stiff and delicate as the few early flowers in the garden border.

'I hope you'll come. I'm singing a few of my own songs,' pantaloons says.

One of those brief silly encounters, but when I'm back in the sitting-room the chairs don't seem so comfy, the fireplace looks small and sparse.

A travel brochure showing a view of Torremolinos—sand, bikinis, concrete egg boxes, sun umbrellas, a blue pool—has been left on the window-sill. Bridget brought it over to Anne. They are planning to go away together.

'It was all a mistake,' Anne says, referring to Brian. 'He would have left her anyway,' she says, referring to Brian's wife.

It seems that Maxie—the girl with the blonde curls—has taken Anne's place.

'I'm mad with myself because it was I who brought her out to visit the cottage. I knew the minute she set eyes on it—and him,' Bridget mourns.

'You probably did me a favour,' Anne replies.

They wander around the sitting-room, as edgy as two thrushes. I'm on a different planet. Just looking across at them confuses me.

'We'll go somewhere cheap,' Anne says, picking up the brochure.

She is remaining on in Brian's office—for the time being. She can't afford to give up her job right now, especially if she is going to take a holiday.

'How does Brian feel about that?' I ask.

'That's his funeral,' Anne says.

CHAPTER SEVENTEEN

Someone has been inspired to write me an anonymous letter. I give it to May. She thinks what I think. She thinks it's from Edna.

'You are a bad woman,' says the letter. 'God will punish yoy.'

'Yoy', to rhyme with 'goy'.

'It looks like Edna's writing,' May says.

May has grown shabby and careless. She is wearing a baggy pair of trousers that must have belonged to Albert, and a jumper with threadbare elbows. But her house is gleaming and the garden all weeded and planted. 'I've nothing else to do, except my work with the pro-life crowd,' she'd said.

But then I remember Mrs Kenny and I think that the letter has come from her. And I drove out to see Betty at the weekend, to beg her to come back to us, but she said she'd be terrified of an infant. 'I'd be sure to drop it,' Betty said. Maybe Betty sent the letter. I think she just used the row with Nancy as an excuse for leaving.

'Are the pro-life crowd going to mind all these babies for us?' I ask May.

'That's not the point,' she says. 'And once they get to twenty you might as well be dead as far as your children are concerned, so enjoy this baby while it is young.'

She is ladling mashed potato and stew onto two dinner plates and one of her sons is coming in the door.

'Is there anything else to eat, Ma?' her son asks, although the stew looks good.

May doesn't seem to mind. 'I can fry you a nice piece of fish,' she says.

Edna couldn't have written any sort of letter. She has shrunk to a wraith since her time in hospital, and her hands shake so much that I don't see how she'll ever be able to mark the ballot paper if she votes in the referendum.

Her house is up for sale. The auctioneer has come out to vet it. He is a pal of Tony's. He is small and plump and wears a camel coat and a flashy brown-checked cap. I wouldn't trust him an inch.

'Where will you go?' I ask.

My question just makes Edna look more anxious than ever.

'I'll be seeing Tony tonight,' the auctioneer says, touching the peak of his fancy headgear with a fat ringed finger.

As he purrs away, Edna runs to her gate and starts yelling after his Mercedes about the slights she has suffered.

I'm the wrong person for this sort of situation. I'm no help at all. I'm about as much help to Edna in trouble as Nancy is to me. 'Oh— Hannah wouldn't be kept in an ice-cream parlour,' Nancy said. 'She's nothing but a little prostitute. A slit in her skirt that goes up to her backside. Sex—that's all she has to recommend her. A young man like Ray who has had the opportunity of a professional education should know better.' Imagine letting Nancy find out about Leo— God! That's another good reason I'll just have to put up with it.

The weather is finally becoming summery. You could go almost anywhere if you had a car and enough money for petrol. I could wear my peeptoe shoes if my feet weren't so swollen. I stand looking down at the only pair of shoes that fit me, green flat things that I picked out of a bargain basket, while Edna's talk degenerates into strange mutters and incantations. As soon as I decently can, I make an excuse about getting to the garage for petrol.

I don't know what will become of Edna. Hidden starvation, I suppose, unless she can get herself attached to some recognised charity. Men in blue suits giving away cheques in smooth envelopes. (Tony does a lot of that sort of thing.) What else can you do if you have never had a job in your life? You are not even qualified for the dole queue.

I'm full to the brim with my own affairs. I can't take the problem of Edna as well.

'Are you taking care of yourself?' Billy Black asks.

'Of course. I'm living like a nun,' I quip, acting the part of a likeable lulu, to keep myself from having hysterics as I lie spreadeagled on his couch.

He pokes around and then nods admiringly. 'Good woman. Everything in the right place.'

Really? I could teach Billy a thing or two that would leave him standing at the post. Then I do have hysterics. 'I'm too old,' I gasp. My face feels brick red. 'Don't be foolish, woman,' he says. 'You're younger than a lot of them, and we'll cut the tubes afterwards so you won't have any more accidents. Hey! I don't want poor Robin sleeping out in the wash-house.'

His words smack against each other and make no sense. Even so, roll on July. I feel as if I've been bashed around until I'm only semi-conscious. I'll have to take up jogging to get myself back into proper shape. Doreen has bought herself a track suit of plum velveteen. She has been sighted by Robin and Jenny, trotting out the Ennis Road. I'm a jelly on a plate. It's an improvement on being a secret drinker I suppose. It's better than loafing around, as Jenny does, looking for mischief.

'Has the overflow stopped?' Billy Black offers a box of tissues.

'I don't know why I've gone through all this,' I say. There was never any compulsion for me to see it through. I'm not so dumb that I couldn't have arranged a quick trip to a London clinic.

'You can tell Robin you'll be as good as new,' he says.

I asked the priest in confession if I should tell my husband that I had been unfaithful to him. He said that there was no moral necessity for me to do so. My sin has been absolved and that should be the end of the matter. Really?

I suppose that they have been watching *Psycho* in hundreds of sitting-rooms this evening. Did anyone else ever think that it was a fantastic film? Once upon a time I did. How young I was! How did I ever swallow that wise-cracking psychologist who sums up everything in the final reel? Even his voice is phoney.

I go out into the garden to recover from the Jewish ham. Imagine a session in that guy's consulting rooms (or his mother's). He certainly does make a nutcase sound easy to crack. Give me a good Catholic confession any day, or give me Dr Billy Black with his, 'There's nothing to having a baby. You know that, Angel.'

I look up and down the road. Deserted. There is nowhere to go but back into the house. I'm sick of the house. Looking at it critically, I can see chunks of dirt forming in the cracks, a film of grease over the kitchen. The lavatory is like the 'ladies' in a bad country pub. I tried to clean the windows this morning and nearly passed out in the attempt.

The evening smells of cut grass. I have left the front door of the house open. I can see the shape of Anne's travelling bags in the hall. She and Bridget are off to Torremolinos tomorrow. I had a postcard from Geraldine yesterday with a picture of the Tower of London on it. I wonder if Leo is back from San Francisco.

Oh, I wish I could keep everything as it is by simple acts of cooking, washing cups, washing my hair. Oh, I want to stop the mad flow, stop it happening. A shot rings out in the soft air, there are flappings, shouts, laughter. Someone was frightening the pigeons. Don't they know that it's strictly against the law.

For a girl who is going off on a carefree holiday, Anne is in a continuing bad mood. I knock at the door of the bedroom. When I go in she is sitting on the edge of her bed, hugging herself and scowling at the Beatrix Potter wallpaper. A novel, with the usual naked bodies on the cover, lies face downwards on the blankets.

'What time are you leaving?'

'Haven't you heard the news?'

'No. All I saw was that stupid film.'

'There's an air-controllers' strike in Shannon. It's causing havoc.'

If that's all I had to worry about! 'So—why don't you change your mind and contact Brian and talk things over.' I toy with the notion of getting in touch with him myself, of attempting, at least, to set someone else's life in order.

'Oh, stop,' Anne says.

After a drugged and troubled night's sleep it is more a matter of coming to than of waking up. I have to stand perfectly still beside the bed until my head stops reeling.

Anne has left her bedroom door open, and the sheets and blankets are neatly folded on the mattress. Downstairs her bags are gone from the hall and I find a note saying that she and Bridget have gone out to the airport to try their luck. I feel disappointed.

I go through the usual routine of orange juice and toast in a semi-coma. The baby is wedged in an awkward diagonal position. It kicks when I take my first swallow of orange juice as if it finds it revolting. Feeling spiteful, I drain the glass as fast as I can and hope it makes the child feel as horrible as I do. Only another few weeks and we'll be rid of each other.

And then the next step will be the christening. Oh, these ceremonies —the seriousness of the men. Everyone standing around with pious faces while Monsignor turns Leo's baby into a Roman Catholic. Holy Wars have been fought over less. I must force myself to remain meek. I can imagine them all rocking back on their heels, if I spill the beans, feeling as if they have been knocked out by Mohammed Ali. Feeling as bad as I feel now. It would only take me two or three minutes to blow it all to smithereens—the silver vessels, the wine, the bread. But I'm not a theologian. I'm prepared to indulge their mistaken beliefs.

I go creeping upstairs to call Robin and Jenny.

'Q: "Who made the world?" A: "God made the world." ' That was about as far as my theological studies ever went. Most of the time I was outside the door with the other culprits who had been trick-acting and passing notes.

'I hate my father's companion.' I stared at the stripy matting on the study floor and wondered if I'd ever have the courage to tell the priest that in confession. And if I did, would he absolve me if I couldn't stop hating her right away? Poor old Bel. Mostly I've kept out of the path of the clergy, put a safe distance between myself and their croziers and condemnations. Just as Bel did I suppose, and everything worked out for her in the end. Last rites, the lot. I stay well away from the centre aisle, with my head bowed while He is being carried past because, after all, a blessing won't go astray. I'm not foolish enough to invite the wrath of God on myself.

The baby kicked all last night and the night before that and some of the day in between. Now it is so quiet that it is just a vague puff, something I've imagined, like my 'friend' Noelle. It just lies there, pampering itself at my expense. How are you doing, kid? Don't you feel up to it? Are you stuck?

However, there's no point in my questioning the certainty of your existence. You're there alright as I skim through the letter columns in the *Irish Times*, where the coming referendum for the protection of the unborn child is throwing up shoals of queer fish. Poets and sons of poets, supreme knights, third-century rabbis, Irishwomen who have had abortions, women having hypothetical children, doctors being driven into premature senile decline, fertilised human seeds, and so on and so forth.

Let's call the whole thing off—eh! I'm more puzzled at the end than at the beginning. The hardest thing of all to grasp is the fact that it was Leo who made me pregnant.

Of course they're all going to romp in—the unborns. Romp in or romp out, everyone of substance is backing them. Robin has given a hefty donation and Leo supported the campaign right from the start. And at grass-roots level there are people like May. They're stronger than the ones against it. Nothing for a woman who has got rid of a baby illegally to do, except keep mum—and someone in my position likewise. My reasoning isn't that woolly. I've got my own cause to protect.

I suppose that the predicament I'm in is exclusively mine, or as scarce as Protestants making novenas. No point in looking for enough soul sisters to form a massive protest—against what?

'Ouch!' The baby has just kicked me in the teeth!

It sometimes creeps up on me like that, takes me by surprise, so that I can't focus—my emerald ring seems to have shattered and become mixed up with the pieces of a broken green shampoo bottle. I begin to pick up the pieces. I just hit my head rather badly, against the washbasin. This pulls me up short. I'm getting increasingly absent-minded. Forgetting to put my teeth in! That was one of Mr King's irritating habits. I used to find them here on the bathroom shelf, or beside his plate when dinner was over. Awful looking objects, combined with a depressing fragility. While he sat chomping with sunken gums, and doleful eyes.

Anne rings from the airport. She's off. Off, with her eyelids swollen and her forehead throbbing from misery, to somewhere over the rainbow.

CHAPTER EIGHTEEN

Although the weather has grown quite warm I spend a lot of time indoors. When I expose myself to the elements I feel as if the sun is shrivelling me up, making me wizened before my time. I sit on the bedroom armchair watching the flies scribble their dances on the windowpanes.

A priest asked me if I'd like some help when he saw me struggling with the door of my car this morning. That's a sure sign that a woman is looking hopeless. I hate these unsolicited Christ-like advances. It made me irritated, particularly as I imagined that he eyed my belly with reverent awe, as if he linked it up with those crude SPUC posters. Society for the Protection of the Unborn Child—leave me alone, this is my business.

So much needs doing in this shack, but I'm in no mood for housework. It's not as if anyone is going to call to see me. My only social encounter these days is Billy Black, and that's in his scruffy surgery, not out in that Titania's palace where Peggy puts a plastic apron on over her georgette dress and labours like a kitchenmaid when all the guests have gone home. Let the odds and ends take care of themselves, ignore the nagging pain of an unkempt house.

'There's no need to clean down the cooker,' I say to Jenny.

'I shouldn't have to do it,' she says darkly.

'What it mostly needs is a Brillo pad,' I say.

She doesn't reply, but keeps digging away with a sharp knife.

What the kitchen needs—taking a hard look at it—is a bomb through the roof to furnish a good reason for the disorder.

'Mushrooms!' Jenny says furiously. She points a rubber-gloved finger at the narrow space between the cooker and sink.

I can't shake off the torpor. I don't think I'd give a damn if it was the mushroom cloud itself springing up through the floorboards. Come on, the sunshine is streaming in the window and the back door is open. Leave the tough jobs. Someone will push the button sooner or later and it will all be taken care of. 'What's that you're using?' I pounce on the washcloth which lies on the floor.

'It wasn't me who tore it up. It was Anne—Anne!'

Like Cinderella when the clock struck, I toss the remains of my good silk shirt back onto the ground.

I've had enough of kitchen-sink drama. I leave the house and walk up the road as far as the pier which gives a view down the river. Not a boat in sight, only the screaming gulls and the usual cormorant. And no mushroom clouds, only, over in the distance, the cement-factory chimneys having a leisurely smoke. I always pushed the pram around the whole circle of the road and then ended up sitting here for a while before going down to cook the tea. Once I was frightened by a mad whiskery old man in the bushes. Once Ray found a bird's nest with eggs in it. Today there are two young people sitting on the grass who say, 'Hello, Mrs King.' Their voices are very slurred. I don't look too closely in case they are drugged and I know their mothers.

'We can't all be like you and Dada,' Anne said before she headed off for Spain. I was shaking out my fur coat to guard against moths laying eggs. I told myself once again to hold on, take it easy.

I move away from the kids on the grass. The man coming towards me is obviously an American. If he's not an American he's wearing pyjama trousers—red-and-white tablecloth check. (Robin wears poplin. I don't know about Leo.) Check trousers and myself peer at each other as we pass. I say 'Hi!' and so does he.

A splash of rain big as a pigeon's dropping lands on my skull from nowhere. Then another, then several. One short excursion on a hot day and I have to get caught in a deluge. I haven't the strength to move fast—check trousers passes me at a gallop—but at least I'm living near at hand. The two druggies stay behind, still sitting on the grass. By the time I reach the house my body aches all over. Those kids are going to catch pneumonia.

'You won't have Angel's problems now,' Edna says.

Doreen, lying against her pillows, flinches as if she has received another knock. A gang of women are gathered in the hospital room. Edna asked me to bring her here to visit Doreen, who has had a hysterectomy. It is generally agreed that the trouble was brought on by her foolhardy jogging. Even so, I feel a stirring envy. It's all over for Doreen no matter what happens.

It is a close quarrelsome day. Polite coughs are spiced with antagonism. The hospital paraphernalia—drip, temperature chart, tubes, steel vessels—stir the arguments.

One of the visitors has nursed in England. The inevitable demands were made so she couldn't stand it any longer. Part of her duties consisted of helping at terminations. 'They make a point of making Irish girls do it. If you'd seen the things I've seen in bedpans, you'd all vote in favour of the unborn child.'

Edna had a sister, whom none of us knew, who died down in Cork, because she was suffering from cancer. No one would give her the necessary medical attention because of her unborn child, which didn't survive in any case. There are a few seconds after Edna has spoken in which we listen to Doreen's rough breathing.

I ache all over.

I guess some people would kill you and me to keep out legislation that favours abortion.

'My father fought in the Civil War. He didn't speak to his only brother again as long as they lived. At their father's funeral he was only allowed to come to the church, his brother barred him from the family house.' May's voice is as hard and dry as a wooden splint.

I wish everything would stop. I'm trying to stay on the fringe. Edna looks as if she is going to have a nervous relapse. She is a thousand years too old for that Indian dress. She puffs her cigarette so fast that a woolly coil of smoke winds around her head, until someone opens the door for ventilation. That makes the room cold. But the arguments remain heated, everyone gobbling like cornered turkeys, while Doreen just lies like a piece of discarded meat. We're all unsuitable. May looks ridiculous in blue trousers, blue jeans in fact. As for me—don't think about it. Doreen's country cousin— the woman who nursed in England—pulsates in a velvet costume. I press my shoulders against the back of my chair and wonder if

Doreen would give me a few of her sleeping pills. I'm afraid to ask Billy Black for more.

'You're looking fine,' I insist when Doreen catches my eye. My ragged smile fools neither of us.

May grabs my arm and pulls me out of the flux of visitors. 'Poor Angel, you'll soon be over it. I want to thank you for that Sunday—you were so kind. You and Robin.' Her breath whistles unpleasantly in my ear.

'It's great to see you all,' Doreen says weakly. 'It takes my mind off all this.'

We know—the drip, the bottles, the chart, mass cards strung along the head of her bed.

The wardsmaid coming in with tea, toast and corned beef on a tray—a signal for us to leave.

'All the home comforts.' May is the first on her feet.

'Try and get it all down this time, missus,' the wardsmaid says.

'Come on, all you pro-lifers.' May leads the way into the passage.

Anne orders us two brandies and white. Her hair is a blonde shimmer, her dress the same soft red as the lounge curtains, her new sandals and painted toenails as red as a wild duck's feet. She is very brown.

Her holiday with Bridget was one hilarious comic strip—in every sense of the word. 'No one wears tops. After the first few minutes you take it for granted that you're topless.' And she had the greatest stroke of luck. She made this fabulous contact. It looks like she has a good chance of landing this super job. All these snippets are tossed at me like golden coins. Anne is happy, she feels generous, she wants to share. And could we keep her belongings until the new flat is fixed up? Yes, she definitely prefers to move in with Bridget. She catches my wrist and says, 'Of course I'll come and baby-sit.' As for Brian, he is just a memory. She will be wiser next time.

In spite of myself I am relaxing, I am laughing with her.

'And I must tell you this—we met a fellow one night—he is connected with the theatre. Dracula's grand-nephew or something.' Anne is off into another fit of laughing.

My brandy glass is empty but Anne's is still untouched.

'We ended up with him reading our horoscopes at three a.m. We nearly slept it out and missed the plane home.' She is still laughing.

Horoscopes or tea-leaves. I don't like mumbo-jumbo.

'What is it, Nancy?' I asked. 'One of my headaches,' Nancy said as she dried the cup and put it on a hook. The red dress was a mistake, too young for her. It drained the last scrap of colour from her face. Nancy often makes mistakes—there was a black and white coat that turned her into a walking chessboard, and a dress decorated with butterfly bows. Another time, I remember a yellow turban that made her sallow. But she never made mistakes with the teacups.

The bar is now very full. No recession here. I'd like to move, especially when a strange man with narrow gold spectacles insists on squeezing into the seat beside me. His fingers are a dirty yellow. Any minute now he'll start to smoke. I'm absolutely roasting but I can't take off my jacket because underneath I'm a show. The result is that I feel sleepy from the heat, so sleepy that I can't stop yawning even though it was my suggestion that Anne take me out for a drink.

God! I suppose that everything has it's funny side. The invisible enemy strikes again. I'm dying to get out of here, but propriety nails me to the seat. I take the precaution of keeping my hands folded in my lap, neat as Bel's in her coffin. I could do with rosary beads. I concentrate so hard on Anne's face that it makes me dizzy and she starts to brush it with her fingers as if she suspects something wrong. Why don't you light a cigarette, sir? To do so you will need to remove your dirty yellow fingers from my knee. I'm pretending that you're not there. That's a black widow spider crawling up my thigh, take care it doesn't get you. Anne can't see anything, even though your filthy hand almost made it that time. I'm finding it difficult to keep up the small talk. I just waffle along. I couldn't bear a scene, accusations. 'The woman is mad!' His moustache atremble with tainted disgust. This must be a new perversion. I'm afraid to look sideways because I know what you're yanking out of your fly.

'They're ghouls,' Anne says.

We're sitting in my car in the carpark, with our noses pointed for home. We've been at a coffee morning in aid of handicapped children. A lopsided gingercake lies on the back seat.

'How can you stand these affairs?' she asks.

She can't wait to be back in an office. Everyone has been looking for news from her. 'Where are you living now?' 'Did I hear that you got engaged?' Poisoned tongues.

'I have enough money to manage,' she says. 'Or I will have after I've got my first pay cheque.'

She is still waiting to hear from the contact she made in Spain. When I ask for more details she is vague, then begins to prattle about something, as if she is afraid of the silence.

It is such a lovely day, too lovely to be miserable—and queasy. I cannot decide whether it is strain or the start of something. It is only a matter of a week or two. Anne's problems, Ray's vagrant life, Jenny's grumpiness are no more than fringe distractions.

The coffee morning wasn't so bad. The woman who sold me the gingercake wore a hat exactly like a saucepan. Upside-down, the way the baby is positioned, poised for its journey.

'Even so, Dad and I—we would like to give you a loan of money.'

We? I squared it with Robin. He said, 'I want a guarantee that we'll get it back.' I said, 'For goodness sake, she's your daughter. However, it's up to you.' He said, 'She's not a baby; she'll have to learn to take care of herself.' 'She needs help.' 'She's not pregnant— is she?' That was sprung at me. No. Let it be, I'm the one who is pregnant. I'm the one who must be protected from the harsh world. Myself and my brat.

'I'm really sorry about landing all this yoke on top of you right now,' Anne says. 'But honestly, I've seen the bank manager. There's no need to worry.'

That's how it is when you are a nice young girl with a good qualification. The bank manager and his computer show their appreciation.

'Well—that's it so,' I switch on the engine. I suppose the baby is frightened by the sudden roar.

I'm choked to the gills. I never wanted any of this. Give me a room in a convent—the smallest, highest attic—nothing to see except the bare sky through the skylight from my narrow bed. One almost as narrow as the crucifix nailed to the wall. The nailed figure, nailed to the wall, the new testament on the one frugal table. The sky a fraction darker than the white plywood furniture. Rise at five-thirty, breakfast at seven, no speaking during recreation hour. 'You'd never make it as a nun,' Bel scoffed, they wouldn't be able to get you out of bed in the mornings.' 'She can be whatever she wants to be.' My father stroked my hair. 'And you're too greedy,' Bel said *sotto voce* as I took the last slice of cold tea-brack.

We drive past the nursing home. The curtains look grubby. One twitches in the room reserved for me. It is average as nursing homes go. The smell of cabbage seems to seep from the floor coverings although I never remember cabbage on the menu. The food is quite pleasant, better than a hospital. A lump of butter melting into your mashed potatoes. You've lost so much bulk in the big push that you don't give a hoot about calories. Cold meat and salad on a steel tray and a big tumbler full of milk to get your own milk flowing. I quarrelled with Robin because he hadn't come near me for twenty-four hours. I threw a tomato at him. He had gone out with the lads instead. 'The lads'—Albert, Paul and Tony. God bless the mark.

I had to stop nursing Jenny because a window was left open and I caught a filthy cold. I lay, sneezing all day, with my breasts growing full and hard as a pair of monster turnips, while nurses coaxed her to suck through a rubber teat. Maybe these early separations affect the mother just as deeply as the infant. At least I know my entitlements by now. The windows will be kept closed, the child lifted into my bed at whatever hour of the day or night I choose. Whatever I say goes, everyone else rates zero—I'm running a one-woman band.

Suppose I die? Everyone thinks that before they have a baby. Suppose I die—like my mother did? It is the nearest you can get to any sort of intellectual life when you're only the glass holding a ninety-five percent proof human being. You're ready to shatter under the slightest provocation.

'Will Dad be there for the birth?' Anne is pulling my leg. 'Fathers often do nowadays.'

Don't mind her. You're not a glass, you're a bean bag, they can punch away and you just alter your contours to suit.

There's an elderly widower down the road who married a fluffy young dumb-belle half his age. Last year, when she produced a child, he stayed with her until the time came when the doctor had to grasp the infant's head with a forceps. 'It was an experience, I learnt a lot from it,' the widower said. I met him at a Christmas party and, although we are only nodding acquaintances, whiskey had brought him to the stage of opening his soul. 'I'm sixty-two and I never saw worse, though my first wife had six of them, God rest her. The force of it, and the mess. I nearly fell dead at the doctor's feet.' He was wearing a pink paper hat because of the Christmas season and it made him look older than Santa Claus. I was getting suspicious about my own condition at the time and I was so tired that I insulted him by yawning in his face. Next time we met he didn't salute me.

CHAPTER NINETEEN

The weather forecast has been wrong as usual. It was supposed to rain this afternoon but the sun shines with an emphatic brightness, the sky is an immaculate blue. All the objects in the garden stand out as distinct and clear as ideograms. Grass, geraniums, greenhouse, toolshed roof, sunbed, red rose, yellow rose, rake, wheelbarrow, my own malaise.

Jenny has just gone into the house after delivering a lamentation about her exams. It serves her right. She should have studied. And she is bold, and cheeky to boot, saying how anyone who has to live under conditions like hers could not hope to pass exams. She planked herself in front of me as aggressively as Andrea Jaeger facing Billy-Jean King across the Wimbledon tennis net. 'Fifteen-love.' The commentator's voice floated through the open window next door all afternoon. If they think Billy-Jean is old how would they rate me? 'Go away,' I said to Jenny so she turned and lurched towards the house. Her unsteady gait reminded me of my poor car. We took it to the garage this morning.

Yesterday a letter came from Ray saying that he has had a great piece of luck, but that he won't be able to come home before he leaves for Germany. He is going to work in a factory over there. 'I think it is the best thing to do,' his cramped slanty writing spelt out. He needed his passport pronto. 'I'm surprised that they'll let him in after being in a kibbutz,' Robin said. There was no mention of Hannah. Also, he would like to say thanks to Mr Abrahamson, and sorry he didn't call. 'I think he's off his head,' Robin said. Robin hates the idea of a summer job in a canning factory. 'Leo was the man to fix him up.' In the afternoon I went to the post office and registered the envelope containing Ray's passport while the postmaster gawked at my ungainly hulk. (Keep looking, mister, and my knickers will fall down.)

When I came out, the car, as a punishment for my bad thoughts, wouldn't start and I was reluctant to go back in and ask for help. I decided that home was within walking distance. The temperature was in the seventies. (In fact we are having a heatwave.) No matter how hard I tried everyone overtook me. A black man wearing a sports jacket nearly knocked me off the footpath. The Russian airmen, who lodge up the road, came along in a jabbering group, swinging supermarket bags. They had left off their leather jackets and black berets. Even my ears were sweating as I trudged and trudged.

I spotted Doreen approaching cautiously from the opposite direction. She was accompanied by a stranger. Not just any stranger—as soon as we got close enough I recognised our whiskery friend who came to my assistance in the library. Doreen looked worried. When she was within earshot she called, 'We have just been sitting in the garden,' as if she was afraid that I might think they had been in bed. 'You couldn't stay indoors on a day like this, Angel,' she said in a mincing girlish voice. I noticed the way that Whiskers moved to a respectable distance when they stopped walking. 'You know Mrs King,' Doreen said. Whiskers bowed. '*Enchanté*.' He carried the usual book as well as an old and grubby raincoat. *Enchanté. Enceinte*. I pleaded haste. '*Au revoir*.'

On top of all this I had forgotten to bring enough money to buy bread for teatime. At this stage you wobble so much that every step is an assault on your efforts to hold yourself together. Doreen and her companion were just one more drain on my energy. What a combination, and Doreen just out of hospital! I tried to imagine Doreen and Mr Whiskers performing any act that wouldn't be suitable for a school concert, but the mind boggled.

Of course I should have asked for help—begged Doreen and her companion to flag down a car, gone back to the post office and called a cab. I must have been in serious danger of haemorrhaging. By the time I reached home I had developed a limp. My feet felt as if dogs had bitten them. I had reached the limit.

Robin was furious instead of sympathetic. What had I been thinking of? He affected a scornful disbelief. 'You actually want to make things as difficult as possible, that's about the size of it. I hope it hasn't harmed the baby.' He said this along with several other expressions of goodwill.

In the evening the crows had a fight in the trees. I was sitting on the garden seat, solacing myself with a brandy while Robin grimly mowed the grass. The birds gathered like a conglomeration of more bad thoughts. There was a second's hush in which everything began to shrink, even my womb tightened as if the baby was trying to protect itself. Then all hell broke loose as the birds swooped and swirled. Their cawing was the most frightening part, a fiendish din. I rushed indoors and sat quaking on the armchair furthest from the window.

This morning I had to steer my car at the end of a rope which was tied onto Robin's back bumper. It was risky but I didn't care. Bulldozers, lorries, men digging, an ESB van, all got in the way. It seemed as if the whole city was in a state of upheaval and breakout while I remained sluggish flesh imprisoning sluggish flesh.

Tears come to my eyes. The noise Jenny is making in the kitchen sounds like a carefully structured insult. Slam, crash—she must be throwing saucepans. I figure that a girl who can't make up a packet of instant stuffing, mix it with chutney, and produce a perfectly satisfactory cracker sandwich doesn't deserve to pass any exams. I'm not wallowing in misery, but how can I buy food without transport?

I've no room left in my head for Jenny's vagaries. She reminds me too much of myself when young—hypocritical and extreme, always looking for objects of scorn, looking for new ways to rule out Bel, prove she was only a back number.

Now I'm the next thing to a back number myself. The baby is sucking away all my heart's blood—manipulating me, making me eat oranges, making me drink glass after glass of iced water, emptying my bladder at frequent intervals, seeing that I keep body and soul together. Giving me a toothache. I should have visited the dentist months ago. I had a wisdom tooth extracted when Jenny was ten days old. It was worse than having her. If it wasn't for the baby I'd stop in my tracks the way my car did and let them tow me to the scrap yard. Then Robin could do whatever he liked.

I squint up my eyes and see with voyeuristic certainty Geraldine's naked breasts and Robin's erection. A tango called 'Jealousy' is playing from my past. The music stops but they continue to sway. I hate being shut out but all I can do is send my ghostly breath in a sad whistle through the keyhole.

'It cuts both ways,' I kept telling myself after I had gone the whole hog with Leo. I was baffled to discover how Leo could be of such little consequence, especially when he had given me such intense pleasure. He hardly means anything now in spite of the moans he drew from my very core, the trouble he went to hunting the last concealed delicious quarry which I had not even known was there myself. 'How many men have you slept with besides Robin?' he asked. 'Hundreds,' I said. 'They must have all been boors,' Leo continued to stroke my clitoris. 'They weren't circumcised,' I said, staring at his cock to hide my confusion.

I chew on a blade of grass and try not to feel too nervous. I have landed myself in a proper shambles. Grass, greenhouse, geraniums, toolshed glinting in the sun—say something, say something, tell me it's all a charade.

Robin and I had a serious conversation shortly before I slept with Leo. We talked about Paul and Geraldine and the accident, and whether we would be wise to let Ray leave college and travel. After we had talked for a while the conversation began to centre almost exclusively on Geraldine. I saw the fire begin to dance in Robin's eyes. I felt that it would swallow everything—bed and board, our whole existence together.

I confronted him with the inescapable fact of my constancy. I even went right back to the beginning, to our interrupted honeymoon. I reminded him of our amateurishly painful attempt at sex with my menstrual flow staining the sheets while back in Ireland my father was dying with only Bel to watch him go. I accused Robin of being glad to get rid of me even then, of having designs on the luscious Roman girls the minute I left the *pensione*. Robin tried every excuse to head me off but I grew relentless. I was prepared to fight fire with fire, apply a scorched-earth policy right back to our cradle days. 'Even when we were kids Bel used to say that you were wishy-washy, a mother's pet,' I said. 'I always stood up for you. I hope you were able to stay the course with Geraldine.

She likes men that can keep up a bold front, if you'll excuse the expression, when she's having a fling. I know, she told me.'

Sometimes, without even trying, you score a bull's eye.

After that there was nothing to do but look for a salve to apply to my own wounds. You could say that I was ready for Leo before I had met up with him at that Dublin function. My initial reaction to his invitation was that the time was ripe.

Oh, I wish I could go back to the beginning and arrange things differently, unsay everything.

'I'll have a ham sandwich,' I said to Leo towards the end of my last visit. I saw again an expression of polite dissatisfaction. As well as my ham sandwich, we each had four drinks in thirty minutes and I was so woozy when he put me on the train that I had to go to the toilet and be sick before it had pulled out of the station. I had mopped my face with Coras Iompair Éireann's bile-green paper towel, and felt, as I feel now, like a condemned criminal. 'You and I could make things hum,' Leo had said, and after five heady weeks we ended up in a square black room in a dowdy pub with nothing to say. Then, 'Safe home, Angel. It has been nice.' I replied casually. I was even dressed casually, in the style of last autumn — layers of wool, a long scarf, my best boots, a silk shirt. It was quite simply the friendliest goodbye we could manage. My chief emotion was gratitude that he hadn't stayed around long enough to interfere with my vomiting. It was only when I realised the horrible pickle I was in that I even thought of attempting to see him again.

I had been so awful to Robin that I was amazed when he was prepared to touch me. I had been an incredible fool. The moment we came back from Rome I acted like a changed woman. I received Robin's tentative advances with desperate encouragement. I used every tantalisation I could think of. I hoped that the baby would co-operate and arrive a little on the late side. 'We never did that before,' Robin said in an awed voice when I tried a trick or two which Leo had shown me. I goggled at him. Was he actually being fooled? Apparently so, but I had to move fast. What a pity, after all, that we had refrained from making love in Rome. There I had insisted on Robin sleeping in the other bed, refused to try any substitute for full sex, taken a wicked delight in seeing him look like a child with his nose pressed against a toy-shop window. 'I'm not ready. I'm not a slot machine,' I had said in Rome.

Although perhaps it was just as well, perhaps that crazy abstinence helped to rekindle our own fire. The time from October to Christmas was the colour of happiness. It was as if we were reinventing ourselves, creating a new Mr and Mrs King, fresh as paint, begun from scratch. It was as if our original semi-ignorant childish beginnings had been shrugged off. But we were only fooling each other.

How long it would have lasted without the baby can only be guesswork. All I have left in my bag of tricks is the baby, I haven't even a leg to stand on.

'Hi!' Anne is standing over my chair. She has had a marvellous time in Dingle. She is bringing the rest of her belongings over to Bridget's this evening. Her new job is all fixed up. 'I brought you a present.' She hands me florists' roses, incubating in a cellophane wrapper, pink and tight as a newborn infant's bum. 'It's an occasion,' she says.

Time kaleidoscopes. Anne is the baby with creamy skin and a button nose. 'Are you looking after yourself, pet?' I ask. I'm so glad to see her.

'Come inside.' She has to haul me out of the chair.

We sit at the kitchen table, drinking warm white wine from glasses salvaged by Anne from the clutter on the draining board. We drink carefully because of their chipped rims. (Geraldine and I used to drink white wine on hot afternoons, both of us getting giggly in her back garden.)

When we went to Rome last October Robin started drinking double whiskies in Shannon airport so by the time we were unpacked he was too sloshed for the fountains. It was our first argument, the next one was over our breakfast croissants, the next when he wanted us to share a bed.

I know the house is a mess, but it is nothing compared to the wear and tear on myself. 'I'm completely disorganised now that the car is gone,' I say, as if that explains the cigarette butt lying in a puddle of milk.

Anne picks it up with a paper towel. 'There are some things I can't take,' she says.

Jenny must be smoking. The cigarette wasn't mine. The shopkeeper should be arrested for selling them in singles. I'm getting very untidy but there is no point in apologising to Anne. When I called round to see Geraldine on the night of the accident I expected to find blood all over the place, but by that time everything had been cleaned up.

'I don't know whether I'm alive or dead,' I say to Anne.

'You're looking great,' she says.

Later still, Robin and I walked along an antiseptic corridor with walls painted the colour of slime, a paddle fan seemed to be whirling inside my head. The ground crunched like a layer of snail shells beneath my feet.

'I feel only fit for a funeral,' I say.

'Don't talk like that,' Anne says.

According to Jenny, the girls in her class passed unkind remarks. All I could hope was that the roof might cave in on top of them. I didn't want to go out, even Edna's invitations smacked of charity. It was much better in the hot luxury of Leo's mews, with myself all dolled up. It was all a game, a grown-up game. Leo padded in and stood by the bath. I slid down so that the bubbles would conceal any bulges. I was going to spend the winter losing weight. 'Pure Reubens,' Leo said. Oh certainly, it was much better than sitting at a coffee table, exhibiting myself for sympathy.

'Is it starting?' Anne says nervously.

I shake my head. I don't think so. Not yet.

CHAPTER TWENTY

I thought I was dying when the blood poured down between my legs. 'Now you're a woman. Everyone does, I do,' Bel said. 'How long will it last?' I asked. 'Until you're in your forties.'

But it's not Bel, it's the young nurse. 'This one is going to be a block-buster,' she says.

A pain begins, and grows and grows. Nothing lasts—the British Raj—all that's left, tandoori chicken and nutty rice among the hollyhocks.

The nurse looks too young, only a schoolgirl—like Jenny.

'He never even tried to French-kiss me . . . He never even touched my body . . . I swear to God—he never even touched my face.' When I was fifteen I didn't even know about periods, until they started.

'You're doing fine,' the child-nurse says. She wheels me around like breakfast on a trolley.

Porridge? Croissants? Well, what do you expect—a limousine? Don't be neurotic.

'You wouldn't understand, but no one thinks anything of it now,' that was Anne talking about Brian and herself . . . I should have told Robin everything . . . I'm barely going to make it. Saying to him, 'I've some shopping to do, I'll stay over for the weekend,' my voice a girlish gush.

'She's confused.' Someone is hiding behind a curtain.

Black clothes, Anne and Jenny in black clothes and the white blouse I wore under the black costume that was really my going-away costume which had been sent to the dyers so that I'd have an alternative to the black coat that the Hurleys sent up.

And I call out because I can't stop the pain.

'You're all burnt from the sun, Mrs King.' The young nurse has an older, more experienced-looking accomplice.

I want to tell her that it is because I've been sitting in the sun
wearing a green nightie but the sounds I make are unformed, 'Gr
… gree … nn …n,' like Albert after his stroke. That's right—
stand there smiling as if I'm the comedy act in a free concert …

I wonder how many women have had sex with Leo since last
September.

Young nurse to old nurse, 'Have you told him?'

'He has another patient to see first.'

They're at a luncheon party, chatting over the smoked salmon.

'Want me to stand by?' Robin put my bag down on a chair in
the entrance hall. 'No thanks.' 'Good.' He had to rush—home to
water the tomatoes before going into the office.

The time is nine-o-five.

The time is ten fifty-five. Showdown—'Aaaahh!!!!' A scream
straight from *The Beast with Five Fingers*, and it peters away like
dirty bathwater gurgling down a drain.

'Stop that, Mrs King, or the whole town will hear you.'

And in between, thanks to the drugs, I feel as if I'm as drunk as
a coot on champagne.

I'd switch places with lucky Edna this minute.

'I'm going to Billy Black,' I said to Robin. 'It never dawned on me,'
Robin said stroking his chin …

They have put something with a sour taste into my mouth …

This has been the saddest year of my life. Now it's penalty time.

I'm sweating. I'm sweating, ferns sprout from my eye sockets,
something is caught in my throat. 'Too—hot.'

'You'll never be finished at this rate.' The nurse's hand commits an
act of violence. 'Dr Black won't come back until you decide to be
a good girl.'

She's a new nurse, the other pair have gone off to have their tea.
She leafs through one of the magazines that Anne brought.

'OK?' Anne asked, with an armful of them, looking frightened
and foolish.

'Come on, Angel. Shift that arse of yours,' Billy Black tries to be bracing in a stentorian whisper.

I notice how withered his arms look in the blue T-shirt. I strain and strain but my muscles have gone on strike.

A face decorated with tinted spectacles slithers out of the slow green evening. Black cloth and white dog-collar.

I'm an overwound spring . . . I can't even move my tongue . . . Someone is having a tantrum in the middle distance, squalling her head off. I think that the whiteness over my face is because they've pulled up the sheet and it's all over . . . But it's just the ceiling pressing down.

'Press down, Mrs King.'

And now it is all non-stop noise and talk.

'I thought we'd be here until Christmas.'

I need a handkerchief. Then—I'm walking through a sheet of glass. It turns everyone's hair and eyes into gleaming splinters. It cuts—oh, it cuts, right up and up, gouging deeper. But they don't care. Then it blurs into a red-hot poker. Zig-zag, like a re-run, slicing through and back and through, nothing to spare my stinging flesh. 'People nowadays,' Nancy complained, using glass to slice open a flat fish. It hurts like mad and yet I'm suspended in sloth.

'She's being very silly, doctor.'

And the priest is back. Sure I'd love to be talking about it, father . . . The blaring light shows up the seediness.

'Ring the husband.'

And this in public! I'm on the TV screen in the corner. I can see you!

'I'm convinced,' one bitch says. They slap my face.

I mustn't sleep. Oh, Jesus. I'm one huge white ache.

Where's this baby?

'It killed her mother.' Bel's remark still poisons.

The wardrobe is huge. I look at it speculatively. It is big and solid enough to hang yourself from.

A note on my pillow, 'No more green apples.' Everyone says how inexplicable.

And then I think, so—I'm not dying.

And this isn't the labour ward. Everything has been cleared

away. I'm the only living creature in this twilight.

I can't remember anything at all. It's a roll of blank film.

People. They were all there, and then the anaesthetist arrived.

I cry and cry because I want them to come back and make it happen differently. I cry because I'm afraid I'll go back to sleep again and next time waking up will be worse. I cry harder than May or Edna ever could. I cry because I never saw Bel shed a tear in her life, not even after my father died. I cry until my vision is distorted and all I can see are hideous black shapes that scamper and frisk. And all kinds of horrors come flooding in, and my sinuses are blocked.

What on earth happened? I feel the cuts on my feet from the broken glass. The bed smells of wet rushes and damp rubber. My breasts— ah, my breasts! And the baby is there in the background of everything. The pro-life amendment has been carried. Hurrah!

'How could anyone think of harming them?' May drools over the iron cot.

She has brought me a box of cakes. I lift the lid and see cream oozing too plentifully from their yellow skins. I want to throw up. What I really need is a better bra, a bra made for a cow.

'Now you're fit for the ball,' says a nurse with rosy cheeks and a country accent. She has brushed my hair, and fluffed the frills of my nightie. She has smoothed on cream and dabbed some colour on my cheeks and eyelids. 'Perfect.' She admires me as I lie listlessly against the pillows. 'What does his daddy think of him?' she asks.

'Give me my bag,' I say in a cold voice. When she carries it over I snatch it from her grasp and pretend to be busy rummaging through its contents until she goes away.

Nancy was here this morning. She has come down to take care of things until I'm out of this place. 'Not that I find it convenient, Angel,' she said. It seems that she had to cancel an appointment to have her hair permed.

'I'm not too well,' I say when Robin asks me how I'm feeling. I have rubbed the stuff off my face with a tissue I found in my bag. I know how I look to him—fat, frumpish, shapeless, drab. 'Don't you wish that you could go and live with Geraldine,' I say.

'Maybe I will,' he says sharply.

I'm sorry to hear him say that. I look out of the window. From my bed I can see out into the street, see people struggling along in the heat. Most of them seem to be walking painfully. And a car across the road is jammed between Robin's and another one, a fact I find amusing. 'Look at that,' I say when the driver has crashed into Robin's car for the third time.

'The stupid eejit!' He spirals away, out of my orbit.

I'm not sleeping and I don't want to eat their hodge-podge dinners that taste of soap. All I do is lie and gaze stupidly at the cot between interruptions. Nursing the child is out of the question. Milk oozes drearily from my nipples. Sometimes the thought of Leo flies into my head. Then I remember how thick and ugly I have grown and I think, well—the first thing you must do, Angel, is get back on your feet. After that, suit yourself.

Jenny called but I had dropped off. She sat in the chair for half an hour. 'But she got tired of waiting,' the nurse said.

I lie with staring eyes and feel the painful shrinking of my body under the nightdress. Agony.

'You should be used to after-pains Mrs King,' the nurse says as Leo decomposes in my flesh.

I turn my head and look boggle-eyed at the bottle of champagne on the bedside table.

Robin brings in my wedding ring. I haven't worn it for months. At first my fingers grew too skinny, and in recent weeks my hands and feet were puffy and stiff. Now it fits comfortably again. Anne has some clothes for me to put on. I feel very odd in my dress and high-heeled shoes. Anne's bare left hand pinches the pleats in my skirt. But of course the waistband is too tight, and the material strains to tearing point across the bodice.

'Where's the party?' Robin pretends that I look good.

No, my dear, I'm a wreck. We'll celebrate some other time.

When they have gone I tear off the clothes and luxuriate in the relief of letting myself spread in my billowing nightdress.

But the baby is fine—it breathes, it waves its fists. I watch it constantly. It turns its head at the slightest sound. When it cries its face becomes as flushed as the dawn sky. I don't mind the cries. They don't affect my frame of mind.

My frame of mind is narrow and set, an oblong space that holds very little. A chapter of a novel, a few sentences from a magazine article, the green of an avocado Doreen brought—how it will taste for my supper—some fresh apricots in a paper bag. The smell of a particular perfume. I haven't worn Opium for months. It is madly expensive.

'Is this what you wanted?'

'Yes.' I spray some on my wrist and hold it up to Robin for inspection.

He doesn't bother to sniff. 'I thought you bought some in the duty-free on the way to Rome,' he says.

So I did, my love. But I threw it away, squirted it down the lavatory one afternoon when I was feeling particularly trapped.

Forget the expense. My frame of mind is narrow, but my body feels gross.

'Does he cry all the time?' Robin asks.

Yes. It's true. But what a pleasant noise, a jolly noise, nothing to express horror about. It's like background music, it's better than the stuff that Jenny's record player inflicts on our eardrums. There is absolutely nothing wrong. He was able to keep it up from a quarter-to-eight this morning until lunchtime. He's no fool, and he's beautifully fat, fat and black-haired. 'No wonder you had heartburn—all that hair,' the night-nurse said. 'Holy smoke! Where did you get the black baby?' May asked.

'The news is good, Angel, everything sound as a bell,' Billy Black says, easing his backside onto my bed as the nurse discreetly leaves the room. Billy stretches out his legs and stares at his shoes. 'We were able to do a little job during the delivery. So—you'll have no more problems.' He clears his throat and goes on, 'The way things are—Billings you know—a woman of your age—the natural methods—a hard time.'

As I listen to his words I see that it is all perfectly normal, nothing to be frightened of. So they cut my tubes. There will never be any danger of my conceiving again. But I clutch Billy's sleeve to keep myself from slipping around the bend. I'm not complaining, I didn't feel a thing.

'It's a simple matter during a birth,' Billy Black says.

Just like cutting off a crucial wire in the car so that the engine is immobilised. Isn't that a relief? To know that I'm not a baby machine, to know that I'm on the safe side. I'm in heaven. When we've drunk the champagne we'll go back to martinis, after the apricots I'd like strawberries and cream.

I'm so glad that I kept my mouth shut, didn't tell the exact truth to anyone who would urge me to have an abortion. I'm registering relief, gratitude, as I kiss Billy's hand.

I have no regrets. I hate death, anything to do with dying. I'm glad Ray hasn't come down although I have been constantly expecting him. I don't want to be reminded of Don—or Bel's pale corpse, or any of the unpleasant tangles.

I'm full of hope, I can even face the boiled cod and lumpy potatoes with gusto. Doreen did a novena. Everything helps— every straw. I thought I was on the road to despair, but I'm not— mother and baby are doing themselves well. I've done my own novena, nine months of expiation. Now I want things to be light and funny, I want to make plans. Buy a red sundress, get my hair restyled. Keep promises. 'I promised Noelle I'd pay her a visit.' Such nonsense, as I sat on one of Doreen's antique chairs. Priceless.

But after a few minutes I have no whisk left. I let the pencil and notepad fall, and lie back feeling as if I have carried the squalling child through a holocaust.

CHAPTER TWENTY-ONE

While the baby fattens and cries I review the past year and feel happy because I'll never have to repeat it. I put on my new red dress. My whole wardrobe needs to be refurbished, everything in it looks as if it belongs to the year dot.

My breasts have shrunk back to normal size.

The baby cries and cries. I pick him up and carry him downstairs. Robin has gone off to work. The baby and I sleep in the back bedroom. We don't come downstairs until everyone has left the house. 'Maybe we'll try another trip to Rome—if we can get someone to mind his highness, or perhaps you'd rather go somewhere else,' Robin said this morning when he came in to kiss me goodbye. The prospect excites me as little as a visit to a graveyard.

I don't see many people. May called yesterday. Her most interesting news was that Edna has turned into a complete nutcase who gets messages from God. She also offered to take the baby for a week so that Robin and I would have a break. 'I don't want a break,' I said.

Nancy left almost as soon as the baby and I came home. As a parting gift, in spite of the heat, she cut the grass on her last afternoon. 'I need to get my teeth into something that will drown out the noise,' she said. Afterwards she plugged her ears with cottonwool before lighting a fag. 'I'll come back again when that child is reared,' she said. I hadn't liked her so much for years.

The baby—he feels like my only child. Anne, Ray, Jenny, I have nothing against them, and nothing for them. They belong to a different gang. It's much nicer to be in the kitchen—just myself and the new child—while they whizz off on their lunatic excursions to zany destinations. They can play with fire as much as they like, my attention is fixed elsewhere.

I could barely take time from attending to the baby—he had just soiled another nappy—to listen to Anne's lament yesterday. 'Of all the low tricks!' she protested. It seems that this new job has faded from the horizon. 'The fellow who was offering it belongs to the same rugby club as Brian,' she said as if that explained everything. She stood in a beam of sunlight. I could see clearly that she had been crying. 'I'm getting out of here,' she said. 'I've heard from a crowd in London. I think they can fix me up.'

Billy Black said I must rest up until the autumn, take it easy. So, though I wanted to scold Anne—and I wanted to shout—instead I just sat there flexing my stomach muscles the way I do whenever I have a spare moment. (I'm disgustingly flabby.)

Anne had two plastic sacks full of odds and ends—old photographs, diaries, letters, souvenirs. She wanted to burn them in the garden, because there is no fireplace in Bridget's flat. 'I don't want them floating around on the city dump,' she said. She made the fire while I attended to the baby. He lay in his bassinette, dribbling instead of crying. When I went out to the garden Anne was glooming over ashes. 'What a bloody world,' she said. Her voice burbled with unshed tears. But then she tossed her head and did an impromptu war dance and said, 'I'll fix you something to eat.'

I can't remember what we ate—I know we were out of bread, butter, sausages, meat, sugar, tea, eggs, lettuce, onions—but I know we ate something. By the time we had finished Anne was cheerful. 'I feel a bit of a rat about leaving you after all you have been through,' she said. The baby was crying again. 'None of that old talk,' I said, forcing my lips into a clownish grin. Afterwards she cleared up for me, peeped in at the baby, borrowed Ray's old bicycle from the garage and pedalled off towards, we hope, wealth and happiness.

The baby is never out of my mind for one minute. Baby . . . baby . . . baby. I perch on my bed and fix him with my eyes. Watching . . . watching . . . . A wren on a thornbush. I'm panting as if I have run in a race. Half the people who are brought into mental homes

are as sane as you and I. If they took the baby away from me I'd
go bananas.

And I think how kind I have tried to be, even with Albert—under
the trees—I didn't scream for May and Robin because who could
blame Albert for making a grab at anyone who might help him to
blot out the prospect of the silent box in the dark earth.

Life, this baby is my life. There is no mystery about it, no need
for Robin to be on the hop-around, driving out from the office
three, four, five times a day to see how I am. I'm fine. I am a
monument to family life.

'Our marital troubles.' The term sounds like a foreign phrase on
Robin's lips. 'I was going to leave it until the weekend so that we
could talk properly, but I honestly can't leave it any longer,' he
says. 'Let's go out into the garden,' he insists.

I know that it is because he doesn't want the baby near him. I
pause in the kitchen to empty down the sink the gin and tonic Robin
pressed into my hand. A thick, swampy smell rises from the greasy
walls, the cluttered work-tops. But in the middle, sparkling in a
glass bowl, the baby's bottles are safe and sterile. They strike a
happy note, give a lift to the heart. I hope that Robin doesn't want
to have a row. I am seized with a waggish flippancy. It leads me
to go over and ruffle his hair as he sits on the sunchair with his back
hunched and his face screwed and tortured. What a glorious, sunny
day! I gulp down the water in my glass with gusto. Cheers! Cheers
to us! I refuse to listen, Robin. Farewells aren't possible, you and
I are going to go on forever. 'It has been a pretty grim period, but
it's alright now,' I say. I can't keep the notes of good-humour out
of my voice. This reminds me of one of our childhood games,
'Truth or Dare' for instance, and I'm the questioner. 'Was it your
idea to play this joke to see if I love you?' I ask.

'No. I find it very sad. I've done everything. I have looked for
advice. I've asked a priest in confession. If you want to know, I
feel a complete blackguard.'

Ssh! You poor wretch. I'm not inquisitive. Let's draw the line
right there.

Robin says, 'Financially you'll do well out of it anyway.'

Geraldine's name hangs in the air so plainly that I swear I can see it, printed in large wobbly letters between myself and the greenhouse. But I couldn't mention her if I was paid in diamonds. Instead I say, 'The tomatoes are beginning to ripen.' I feel sick, sick to death. Just because I'm a woman I'm the prey of bad timing, doubtful contraceptive advice, and very questionable medical treatment. 'This is all your fault,' I say. But I don't mean just you, Robin. I mean you, Leo. I mean you, Billy Black. 'Billy Black has tied off my tubes. There won't be any danger of another child. Men. Men. They think they can just walk away,' I say. During the gaps between my statements the baby's cries ring out clear and loud as bells.

Jenny comes padding across the grass in her bare feet. 'What's wrong?' she asks.

'Your father has gone suddenly crazy.'

Robin doesn't lift his head, but continues to stay curled up and withdrawn as a snail in a shell.

'He's had a brainstorm,' I say. After twenty-three years of marriage I am qualified to speak on his behalf. 'He's planning to walk out and leave us.'

The bright flowers in the border nod their heads.

'You're not serious!' Jenny's mouth opens and shuts the way a person's does when a bolt strikes from the blue.

I sympathise. I know the horrid, terrifying sense of displacement you experience when the world suddenly shatters. Did I ever tell you about the time my father died? It's so easy to get mixed up, so easy to mistake motives.

Jenny backs away from me (her face has broken out in pimples), she swings a dirty canvas bag as if it was a grenade—and that's my lurex top she is wearing. 'Oh—oh—you're horrible,' Jenny wails, pointing her finger at me, and then she claps her hand over her mouth.

It's sunstroke. We have all been touched by the sun. Today is a scorcher. Look, I'm going to tear my hair out by the roots to give my brain a chance to breathe. I'm swelling up again, I'm a red balloon. I float after Robin as he gets out of the chair, walks towards the house, clambers up the stairs. I'm in such a state that I don't know what I'm doing. Scarlet dresses are bad luck for me.

Nancy wore one that time she read Ray's tea-leaves. I'm a red rag to a bull as I race around after Robin. But he's too quick for me. My attempt to use physical force is laughable, he escapes with only a scratch on his cheek.

'Clap hands, clap hands till Daddy comes home.' If it wasn't for the baby the place would be a funeral parlour. I shop for the baby and I cook for the baby. I arrange my hair carefully for the baby's sake. I powder my nose after I have powdered the baby's bottom. 'Did anyone ever mention your beautiful nose?' Leo murmured. Fortunately the baby has my nose.

I'm stern with myself and with the baby. All my actions are carried out in a strong, matter-of-fact way. I even carried a very frightened bat with horrible liquorice claws out of our bedroom on the end of a brush-handle without a tremor. I could have been St Joan carrying her sword. I wished that Bel was there to see me— and then I was glad that she was dead.

There are other things that I'm glad about. I'm glad that a niche has been found for Ray in Robin's insurance company, I'm glad that Anne is being brave and that Jenny seems to be behaving herself. They'll get by. I'm glad that Robin looked so miserable in the solicitor's office yesterday.

I kneel on the floor beside the baby's cot as another day dies. I have pinned a Virgin Mary medal onto his blue blanket for safety's sake. He has just fallen asleep and already I'm impatient for him to wake up again so that I can kiss, and touch, and stroke. I dare to place my hand against his cheek and feel its softness.

The only other person I have seen all day is Noelle, my friend from Dublin. When I opened the door I thought for a minute that it was Geraldine, and then I remembered. 'Look!' she said, and held out the little coat she had made. I instructed her to take off her shoes before we went upstairs.

'This room is boiling hot,' she said. But that's the way I want it. I refused to let her open the window. 'Here he is,' I said, and pulled down the blanket an inch so that she could see.

There you lay, my little honey, looking good enough to eat.

I lifted my head. The sweat was running down Noelle's forehead
and into her eyes. I felt hurt because she gave you such a cursory
glance. 'Do you know who I am?' she asked me. Do we know who
anyone is? I nodded my head. 'You're Noelle,' I said. She looked
at me so hard that all her mascara melted. I noticed how lined her
skin had become. It wasn't a friendly face, it was the face of an all-
seeing, all-knowing madame. I thought how good it would be to
push it in with a sledge hammer. She was able to read my mind.
'I can't stay now. You must promise me not to go out. I'll be back
as quickly as I can,' she said. 'Where did you come from?' I asked.
I even had a wild suspicion that Leo had sent her. 'How is Leo
Abrahamson?' I asked cunningly. She didn't answer, but hurried
out, sour as a pickle.

I'm still here, waiting for her to come back, and you to wake up.
I don't mind in the least. While I wait I can feel myself growing
stronger and stronger, strong enough to be the mother of all
mankind.